D0700426

JOHANNES URZIDIL

THE LAST
BELL

Translated from the German
by David Burnett

PUSHKIN PRESS

LONDON

Pushkin Press
71–75 Shelton Street
London, WC2H 9JQ

"The Last Bell" was first published as "Letztes Läuten" in Zurich in 1968

"The Duchess of Albanera" was first published as
"Die Herzogin von Albanera" in Zurich in 1966

"Siegelmann's Journeys" was first published as
"Die Reisen Siegelmanns" in Munich in 1962

"Borderland" was first published as "Grenzland" and
"Where the Valley Ends" was first published as "Wo das Tal
endet". Both were first published in Munich in 1956

First published by Pushkin Press in 2017

1 3 5 7 9 8 6 4 2

ISBN 978 1 782272 39 7

Frontispiece: Johannes Urzidil © IMAGNO/Otto Breicha

Designed and typeset by Tetragon, London
Proudly printed and bound in Great Britain by
TJ International, Padstow, Cornwall on Munken Premium White

www.pushkinpress.com

CONTENTS

INTRODUCTION

I N 1969, a year before his death, Johannes Urzidil recounted an anecdote from his early years as an émigré in the United States. Unable to earn a steady income through writing as a German- and Czech-speaking immigrant in New York, he decided on a whim to try his hand at leatherworking. It happened like this. Visiting a friend and fellow émigré one day, the sculptor Bernard Reder from Bukovina, he spotted a ragged three-volume edition of Rabelais on the artist's mantelpiece. The Baroque-era edition had recently been used by Reder while making a series of woodcuts, hence its sorry state. Urzidil, ever the poor but loyal friend, offered to rebind the precious tomes in pigskin. So he took his meager savings of seven dollars—this was the early 1940s—and went to the leather dealers of Lower Manhattan to scrape up the scarce materials he needed. The writer-turned-craftsman worked hard, teaching himself as he went along, and only when he was done did he notice that the books, though handsome enough to the eye, had basically been glued shut. He presented them to his friend regardless, explaining their sole defect with some embarrassment. But the sculptor shrugged it off with the poise of a seasoned refugee: Never mind, said Reder, they'd served their purpose. The volumes were placed back onto the mantelpiece "between two blocks of marble, where, incidentally, they cut quite a figure, but served as a patent warning to me upon subsequent visits against all too daring exploits and experiments doomed to failure."*

A closed book to the English-speaking world, glued shut and all but inaccessible—this is also an apt description of the writer Johannes Urzidil, a hidden treasure locked away in a language unknown to most of those around him, waiting to be plucked from the mantelpiece, rebound (hopefully this time with a little more skill) and placed into the hands of a new generation of readers. This volume, in other words, is a literary event: the first ever collection of fiction by Prague-born New York writer Johannes Urzidil to be published in English, the language of his adopted homeland.

In a sense, this collection is doubly belated, a minor Urzidil renaissance having occurred in the early 1990s in other parts of the world, with the fall of Communism and the rediscovery of "Magic Prague." Well over a dozen collections of his fiction in translation reached lucky Czech, French, Italian and Spanish readers, but the English-speaking world was sadly overlooked. The present edition is the first step to rectifying this oversight.

* All translations from the German are mine, except where otherwise noted.

Johannes Urzidil was born on February 3, 1896 in multiethnic Prague, capital of the Austro-Hungarian crownland of Bohemia. In 1918 he would witness—and welcome—the founding of the independent republic of Czechoslovakia, followed two decades later by the disaster of Nazi occupation. Forced to flee, he went first to Britain then to the United States, where he lived from 1941 until his death in 1970 on a reading tour in Rome; he was buried at Campo Santo Teutonico, "the Teutonic Cemetery," in the Vatican, adjacent to St Peter's Basilica. Catholic by faith, Urzidil was in fact the eighth child of a Jewish mother who died when young Johannes was not yet four, leaving him and his father with seven older half-siblings from her previous marriage. He later married the poet and daughter of a Prague rabbi, Gertrude Thieberger, whose brother was Kafka's Hebrew teacher. (It was, incidentally, this brother-in-law of Urzidil who related the anecdote—retold by Ernst Pawel—about Kafka looking down at the Old Town Square from Thieberger's window on Karpfengasse, saying, "this narrow circle encompasses my entire life.") Urzidil's father was an ethnic German from the Sudetenland, a patent-holding inventor and railroad official; his stepmother a national-minded Czech from Nymburk, "the poetic realm of Bohumil Hrabal." He spoke Czech and German with equal fluency, though he mainly wrote in German.

Urzidil had already been a published author and journalist in the German-speaking world for over two decades when he was uprooted by historical events. Apart from penning short stories and poems, essays on art, culture and politics, as well as a few biographies, he had also worked for fifteen years as an employee of the German embassy in Prague, even taking on German citizenship in the early 1930s. To the newly arriving Nazis in Berlin, however, Urzidil was nothing but a "half-Jew" (*Halbjude*), whom they promptly dismissed from their payroll. He continued to eke out a meager existence writing for Swiss and Czech dailies until the Nazi invasion of Prague and the "rump of Czechoslovakia" in March 1939. Wanted by the Gestapo for his criticisms of the Reich and its Führer, in the summer of 1939 this prototypically Central European figure from the "literary stewpot" of Old Prague with its "roiling German-Czech-Jewish brew" (as Cynthia Ozick put it), this man with his own "tremendous world inside his head" escaped with his wife using forged passports. In his suitcase, a copy of his friend Franz Kafka's first published book, *Betrachtung*, inscribed by the author; handwritten letters by Stifter and Goethe; a German Bible from 1568; and a Greek edition of Homer's *Odyssey*.

From Trieste he managed to secure safe passage to Britain under the generous sponsorship of fellow writer Bryher (the nom de plume of Annie Winifred Ellerman). After a year and a half in the English countryside near Gloucester, in the village of Viney Hill, he arrived in New York in February 1941. New York City would be his home for the next three decades and would witness the true flowering of this pre-eminent prose stylist, a fiction-cum-memoir writer in German, living in the New World. Though never switching to the dominant language of his adoptive homeland, it was ultimately here, "in the stark shadows of New York skyscrapers and at the same time in the unspeakably bright free light of a new world, hungry for and abandoned to its energetic present," that he found his mature voice in German, often looking back fondly—and critically—at the world he'd left behind. His was no sickly nostalgia. He had no illusions that this was a vanished world. With typical Urzidilian wisdom, he commented on this need to suffer, let go and move on as a natural part of life:

> Should one really yearn for something that is long gone or has meanwhile changed completely? The exile changes too, and all he longs for is his own former self, which wouldn't exist anymore, either, even if he could have remained in his homeland. One shouldn't yearn for the lost beloved. Yet the heart pines for the sorrow of utter disappointment in order to finally find peace.

Indeed, it was a painful disappointment when two and a half million ethnic Germans were expelled from Czechoslovakia in the late 1940s, resulting in thousands of deaths and suicides, as a result of the Beneš decrees (Urzidil had been an admirer and supporter of Edvard Beneš, the president-in-exile of Czechoslovakia, and there are even photos of the two men together). But it was the very irretrievability of his "Lost

Beloved"—the title of his literary breakthrough in 1956 at the age of sixty—that fired his creative powers late in life and earned him the proud reputation of being "the great troubadour of a Prague forever lost," coined by no other than Kafka's greatest friend and advocate Max Brod. Visitors to today's Prague will now find a giant plaque on bustling Na příkopě, in the heart of the city, describing Urzidil as the "last poet of the Prague Circle."

Essentially Johannes Urzidil did the opposite of what Borges advised his fellow Argentine writers at the very same moment in history: "we should feel that our patrimony is the universe; we should essay all themes, and we cannot limit ourselves to purely Argentine subjects in order to be Argentine."* Urzidil turned a world that would be no more, Old Austrian Prague and Bohemia, his patrimony, into a universe unto itself, handling his memories as a rich heritage and treasure. Whereas Kafka barely ever left his "narrow circle" in Prague ("Prague won't let go... this little mother has claws") and wrote a prose that was utterly devoid of place, his younger friend Urzidil had no choice but to be on the move, yet chose to put the bulk of his fiction in an eminently concrete historical setting: Bohemia of the nineteenth and early twentieth centuries. It was this very personal "world of yesterday" that Johannes Urzidil endeavored to rescue from oblivion and recreate in his diverse writing.

---

* From *Labyrinths* (1962), translated by James E. Irby.

Urzidil knew his strengths as a writer and focused on the well-crafted, compact short form. In an essay on Van Gogh from the 1920s, he writes that artistic perfection is not achieved by tackling all-embracing themes but by limiting one's subject (he also cites Dürer and Rembrandt as models, and in another essay refers to Michelangelo's "fragmentarism"). Complexity runs the risk of being spread too thinly across the surface, whereas simplicity has depth. This principle is evident in his own work and his favored genre of the long story or novella. From his stormy, turgid expressionist beginnings, he increasingly achieved an almost classical purity, which late in life gave way to a more leisurely, conversational style, often focusing on small, anecdotal events or moments in his childhood and youth. It is this loving attention to detail that gives seemingly banal or absurd events a deeper significance and sometimes reveals the world to be a place of mystical interconnectedness and continuity. "We all live, I would venture to say, as provisional models of deeper realities, though not everyone has the good fortune to be cognizant of this," he writes in one story in this collection. Far from being mere artifice, a willful tidying-up of the world and its inherent messiness, his stories are taken from observation; their truths are *revealed* to the observant eye and not *construed* by a wordsmith usurping the role of creator. The truth lies in the things themselves.

In an afterword from 1957, he expounded on his poetic principle as follows:

All the people I portray existed, all the events I relate were real in some way […] Maybe, so I hoped, my reality will be of use to this or that reader, and I will touch his heart with mine. There's nothing I've concealed, not the tiniest glimmer of light in the deepest depth of every darkness, not the bitter dregs of every joy. I think I've learned that elements of consolation and cheer resonate everywhere, even among the lost and abandoned.

Urzidil is a realist and religious humanist in one, a writer who never lost his cosmic vision of life's fundamental meaningfulness even in the face of brutality and death. "One does not escape from despair, helplessness, suicide by demonstrating with great diligence and accuracy how nauseating, shallow, stale and fruitless all our actions are, but by trying to believe in life by virtue of the absurd," he wrote in 1965, in a book-length essay called "Literature as Creative Responsibility." To his writer colleagues he once posed the rhetorical question: "Why do you write? Why do you live? In what way do you help others live? They certainly can die without your help."* Fiction-writing, for Urzidil, is an office with an ethical function. Again, one thinks of Kafka, with his almost religious devotion to writing—Kafka the quintessential tortured soul who could only *exist* through his writing, in the hope that it might make him worthy of salvation. And yet the contrast

---

* This and the preceding quote were translated by Wolfgang Elfe (*Dictionary of Literary Biography*, 1989).

couldn't be more stark. Whereas Kafka doubted in his own credibility as a Jew writing in the German language, fearing his creations were a sham, "a literature impossible in every respect, a Gypsy literature that stole the German child from the cradle and hurriedly whipped it into shape, because someone had to walk the tightrope," Urzidil blithely noted, "My homeland is my writing." His writing seems to exude a sense of certainty, the warmth of a well-ordered universe; his style seems downright vigorous and well-rounded (traits reflected in his handwriting as well, as Claudio Magris, an early admirer and promoter of Urzidil, pointed out). Urzidil was assured of his language and his art.

Like Kafka's, his surname is actually Czech. According to a theory put forth by his friend Max Brod, it means something akin to "he put things in good order," an involuntary tribute—*nomen est omen*—to the great discipline and clarity of his poetic vision, his debt to the classics. As in Kafka's case, there is also some debate about where to put him in terms of literary history. Urzidil was an outsider most of his life: as a stepchild, "half-Jew," emigrant, and artist, but also, one might venture to say, as an old-fashioned humanist in an increasingly antihumanist world. His books went against the trends of the day, belonging neither to the politicized literature associated with the much-fêted postwar "Gruppe 47" nor to the self-indulgent navel-gazing, the "new subjectivity," that would come to replace it. Urzidil was a mensch and thinker, a man of letters in search of continuity and order, in nature and *human* nature, immune to the ups and down of politics. He was a literary outlier in purely geographic terms too, living in the United States and publishing in Munich and Zurich. On top of which his original audience, whom he wrote for during the inter-war period, was murdered or driven away. So was he a Jewish writer or a German one, an Austrian or an American? Or simply a "writer in exile," a representative of the vast *Exilliteratur* that resulted from the tragedy of twentieth-century European history?

The poet Mascha Kaléko, another displaced Central European, wrote the following poem in a letter to Johannes and his wife Gertrude sometime in the early 1950s, while she was living in Greenwich Village and the two of them in Queens:

> When I heard the name the very first time
> Back in Berlin—one said Or-tsi-dill
> Was it the foreign sound that beguiled me:
> … A summer evening, blue and starry-tranquil,
> Only from far does one hear the murmur of an Urzidil.
>
> What is an Urzidil? Can one comprehend it?
> Is it an attribute? Abstract… concrete?
> It seems there are no Urzidils in great masses
> And yet you're a textbook example.

Johannes Urzidil himself liked to quip, "*Ich bin hinternational*"— a neologism playing on the German preposition *hinter* and meaning something like "behind nations" or, perhaps more appropriately, among and beyond nations—"at once supra-national and true to his roots," as one admiring critic noted.

I have taken the liberty of gleaning from different collections for this volume, and I think this is not a disservice to Urzidil as a writer. Urzidil wrote and collected his stories as he went along, with little regard for their thematic coherence. "Urzidil's works are all fragments of a single autobiography," Peter Demetz has remarked. And yet the pieces in this collection are unique. Most of Urzidil's fiction writing was in the first person and clearly centered on his own experiences. These pieces, however, shine the spotlight on other characters. Only in the last two selections does the narrator Urzidil intrude, albeit discreetly.

The protagonists of these stories are all misfits and outsiders in some way or another, like Urzidil himself, whose sympathy was always for the underdog. The narrator of the first story, "The Last Bell" (1968), chronologically the last in this collection in terms of both setting and publication date, is the Czech housemaid Marška, the only first-person female narrator in Urzidil's oeuvre, and the rare first-person narrator that is clearly not a thinly veiled Urzidil. Marška is faced with the unexpected when her master and mistress flee the Nazi occupation, leaving everything behind: their worldly possessions, their savings, and a furnished, pre-paid apartment. Needless to say, things go sour when she naively invites her younger sister Joška to come live with her, alas for the wrong reasons.

The unassuming and upright bank clerk Wenzel Schaschek, the rather cranky hero of our second story, "The Duchess of Albanera" (1966), likewise courts misfortune by committing a lone act of daring, utterly out of character for him. (His name, incidentally, means "fool" in Czech.) Richard Siegelmann, too, the bookish protagonist of "Siegelmann's Journeys" (1962), has his routine life as a bachelor interrupted when a female client falls in love with him and the white lie he tells, born of shame and modesty, eventually spins out of control.

But the true outsiders of this collection are Ottilie, the child of nature in "Borderland" (1956), and Alois, the village idiot, in "Where the Valley Ends" (1956). Ottilie—a homage to Stifter's "Abdias"—is the victim of circumstances or, rather, of her uncomprehending surroundings, which can't seem to make her conform to their rules: Instead of praying the "Our Father" she insists on "Our Mother." Her otherworldliness coupled with the confusion of her awakening sexuality drive her to destruction.* Alois, on the other hand, is the scapegoat blamed for a stolen cheesecake that causes a rift in a small Bohemian village and eventually

---

* Hermann Hesse read the story and commented to Urzidil in a letter: "your story about Otti and the Bohemian Forest deeply impressed and delighted me. I thank you very much for that. I once knew a child with similar gifts…" (Letter from Montagnola, December 12, 1955).

unleashes downright warfare—a precursor of the ideological divides that would soon tear the village apart in the name of populism, first from the Right, then from the Left, before nature reclaimed it entirely.

In an essay on Kafka's microstory "The Next Village," a parable of action vs. reflection, Urzidil talks about the grandfather who's astonished by young people making decisions—in this case, getting on a horse and riding to the next village, an inconceivable act of daring for this old man. Urzidil writes:

> What the grandfather, who no longer acts but merely contemplates, can hardly seem to comprehend is the young man's fearlessness and unscrupulousness, his uninhibited ability to come to a decision. The core of the parable, which formulates by way of narrative its lesson and its challenge at once, lies in the concept of responsibility as illustrated by Goethe's maxim: "The man who acts is always without conscience; only the man of contemplation can ever have a conscience."
>
> The parable is his great astonishment. Astonishment that there are people—and apparently the majority of people—who dare to take a decision and carry it out, too, with no fear, reservations or pangs of conscience, people who do not even think to consider the far-reaching ramifications and possible consequences of their decision and its execution, who thus act beyond morality and seem

to do just fine without it; indeed, that life itself—regarded as a happening—actually takes place outside the realm of thought and reflection, indeed must take place there, because only beyond the realm of thought can it have any color at all and be deserving of the name life.

In a way these stories illustrate this very point: that no one can act or *be in this world*, without becoming guilty—a very unmodern, biblical notion in our ideal world of transparency and accountability.

The five well-meaning but flawed protagonists of these five stories—sometimes shrewd, sometimes bumbling—all manage to wreak havoc, more or less unwittingly. And yet these too are lives lived, real and valid stories worth telling. "Human life," a character in one Urzidil story muses, "is long but also short. One can suffer through it or laugh through it, use it to function or leave an impression, but one can also squander it. There is no need to be alarmed by this. Squandering it does not mean living life any less. One cannot, after all, do more with life than live it."

David Burnett
Leipzig, September 2016

THE LAST BELL

I

THIS MORNING, in the wee hours, the Mister and Missus went away. I don't know where to. All they had were their two little suitcases. I accompanied them to the train anyway. Not many lamps at the platform, but a load of policemen and undercovers. You can recognize them a mile away.

"Don't talk too much, and more than anything: Don't start bawling. You'll attract attention."

I knew it would be forever. But I don't know why I wasn't allowed to cry. I pulled myself together. I usually bawl my eyes out at the station, no matter if they're coming or going. All I need to do is walk past a train station and already I start to cry. I feel bad for the ones who are leaving, but I also feel bad for the ones arriving, because they had to leave from somewhere. Goodbyes everywhere! This time I cried on the street, was still crying behind the theater. Some people were just coming out. "Why you crying, miss?" one of them asks me, "the show was hilarious."—"Ten years," I say, "ten years.

The beds in the morning, then the coffee, and every Sunday an egg for the Mister. Then cleaning up, shopping, cooking. Dusting whenever I had a chance: old cups, glassware, books, and so forth; I was always careful that nothing got chipped or cracked. Ten whole years."—"Well," says the man, "that's a long time. But don't you think you've maybe got a screw loose?"—"No. Because suddenly nothing matters anymore. I can shatter everything, tear it to shreds, dirty it to my heart's content. 'Cause it all belongs to me now."—"Is that so? Well then, you're awfully lucky," says the man and continues on his way, as if he'd been frightened.

The Mister called me into his workroom at around nine o'clock. "Listen up, Marška"—he addressed me in the polite form, but was always switching back and forth—"we're leaving tonight. Swear that you won't tell a soul for the next two weeks. If anyone asks, you know nothing. Where to? Somewhere. To tell the truth, we don't even know ourselves. Don't faint on me now. Here's ten thousand crowns. A gift from me to you."

"What for? How come?"

"Don't ask too many questions. Put it in your pocket. It's all we've got, and we're not allowed to take more than twenty marks with us. If they catch us, they'll get us for currency smuggling too. It's all the same in the end, I suppose, but you like to think you're safer by following more of the rules. That's poppycock, of course. But poppycock is what makes the world go round."

"And what about the apartment?"

"Ah, the apartment. You can have that too. It'll make a nice dowry for you."

"What? All the furnishings? The glass cabinet? The porcelain and the antique glassware? The rugs? The Tyrolean chest? The clothing and linens?"

"Stop cataloging. Do what you want with all that junk. The rent is paid for the next six months. That gives you enough time to think it over."

"So you're never coming back?"

"One never comes back, except from summer vacations and business trips, but even that isn't certain. Enough said."

He actually said, "junk." My teeth were chattering. Not because I was happy about the money and all the stuff. But because everything suddenly seemed worthless. Could you call it a gift at all? It was nothing but discarded goods. I'd looked after these things for years, watching each object like a hawk.

"And the books? What's going to happen to the books?"

"Well, you're probably not going to read them. Sell them before they end up on the dung heap. Now leave me alone for a little while." So I went in the kitchen and started to bawl. "Stop your whining," the Missus said, "that's all we need right now." He probably thought I was honest and loyal. Granted, I wasn't the worst. But I wasn't as honest as he might have thought. I really lined my pockets sometimes.

Nobody's a saint, and what fun is anything without a little swindle. Anyway, it all has to balance out somehow.

The Missus could be unbearable at times. Of course she didn't always have it easy, what with all his running around. Men! But even that can have a silver lining. Because the more somebody runs around, the more considerate he can be. Not necessarily, but sometimes. I was always careful with him. There was never any hanky-panky with me. Kind of a pity, actually! But it's not worth it, I know that from my sister. She thought she'd be better off if she fooled around with the husband, but as soon as she was in a delicate condition the husband denied everything and the wife threw her out. She was lucky the child preferred not to come. Joška was only seventeen. That kind of thing shouldn't happen to you. I was much more practical in this regard. As is evidently the case, Uncle Peter used to say.

I'm awfully scared now. What do I say if someone asks me: Where'd you get all that? No one will believe me if I tell the truth. "You should have had it put in writing," they'll say. "Thief," they'll say. The cash I can try to stash away and use up little by little. Not that that'll be easy. If you've got money, you want to feel like you've got it. The furniture, books and things, those are going to be a real pain. But I don't have to sell anything yet. Because, first of all, maybe—Heaven forbid—they'll come back after all; second, I have no clue what any of it's worth, so they're just going to rob me blind; third, I have no need, 'cause I've got enough cash; fourth,

I can always say I'm managing affairs for the master and mistress of the house. In any case, I'll have Joška come live with me. Who could stand to live like this alone? Everything's become so slick. If I touch anything, it'll slip through my fingers. I have to get used to it first, and the things here have to get used to me. I'm no longer in between them and the Mister and Missus. I'm the mistress of the house now. And I have to learn that the ones who don't obey get the boot. Joška is two years younger than me, but cheekier from all the lessons she's learned, a few dozen more than me, I imagine.

I'm one grand richer than I was an hour ago. I found it behind a dresser drawer that used to belong to the Missus. The Mister said the furniture's mine. So anything stashed in the furniture must be mine too. She probably didn't think of it, what with all the commotion. But who ever heard of a woman who doesn't think of her money? She probably didn't have the guts to take it with her. But are there women who don't have the guts when it comes to money? What business is it of mine? Whatever the case, I've got it now. But I won't tell Joška how much and where I got it from. I'll call it my savings, and strictly speaking it's true. I worked here for ten years and was probably worth three times my wage. A pretty penny if you factor in interest and compound interest. So why should I have a bad conscience? Who's got one of those nowadays anyway? True, I still feel a little bit ashamed before I fall asleep. But that'll pass. Everything does. Tomorrow I'll buy myself a couple of new outfits, then

I'll write to Joška. Come and stay with me, I'll say. "With me" because my employers are on vacation, until further notice. How much further, I don't really know. But you can stay a while for sure.

And so I went clothes shopping. Two dresses in two different shops. I tried on five at each and it was worth it. I kept the one with green polka dots and the one with a blue-and-red check pattern. The Missus's things are still in decent shape, but none of them fit me. Maybe Joška can wear them. The salesgirl in the second store was kind of impatient. It was just before closing time, and she was probably in a hurry to get to some rendezvous. But I decided to borrow her time for a while. "Don't treat a customer so rudely." I rustled up a dozen pairs of socks too, and a snakeskin purse in a leather-goods store. I'm a sucker for snakeskin. And I even went to a restaurant. I made it worth my money too. "This roast venison stinks. Send it back to the kitchen."—"It does not stink, madam. It's *haut goût*."—"It stinks, don't lecture me about hoe goo. I'm the customer here."—"As you wish, madam. I'll bring you another portion." The other portion stunk just as bad, but that's the way you have to deal with these people. As long as you've got money, the prettiest roses can stink to high heaven.

The waiter, by the way, looked just like Uncle Peter, who happened to be a waiter too, and was the first one to do it with me, back when I was thirteen. My mother had gone shopping and I was bringing him his breakfast. I was almost naked, on purpose, and so he went all the way with me. I acted like I knew all about that stuff already, and let him do what he wanted with me. I still felt pretty bashful though, most of all for feeling bashful. Uncle Peter noticed and said, "You little hussy." He was killed later on in some brawl. We were having dinner when the news arrived. Joška bawled her eyes out, but not me; I kept on eating my favorite pudding. Mother asked, "Don't you feel the least bit sorry?"—"No," I said, and she slapped me. So this waiter looked like Uncle Peter. I didn't hold it against him though. The apple tart went straight back to the kitchen too. You should always show that you're used to better. That's how you act if you want to be a lady.

I wonder what the Mister and Missus are up to right about now? I hope they didn't nab them. The better sort always seem to find a way out. Mine were pretty decent folks, but only because they weren't too rich. Stasi, who works for the Bockenhauers, told me about their fancy parties, and how at the end they're all completely soused. A real live bank official even followed her up to her room. Who knows all the things he did with her. He gave her a five-crown tip in the hall when he left, and thanked Frau Bockenhauer. "*Küss die Hand, gnä' Frau*—good day, madam, 'twas a splendid evening."

Two plain-clothes Gestapo men came today. I nearly told them: No need to wear those Party badges, gentlemen. I can recognize your mugs a thousand feet away. But I held my tongue. "Where are the Mister and Missus?"

"What do I know? Maybe in the Bohemian Forest. That's where they usually go."

"This time of year?"

"There's no accounting for tastes."

"You might want to lower your voice," one of them snarled, rummaging through the books. "Not a single decent German book here."

"What do you mean?" I ask, "there's nothing but German books here."

"What do you know about books. Are you a *Volksdeutsche*—an ethnic German?"

"Not that I know of. I'm from Moravia. They speak German there too. But mostly Czech. I speak mostly Czech. If I have to, I can speak German though."

"We'll make a good German out of you," said the other one, patting me on the behind.

"You keep your hands to yourself, mister, or I might get nasty."

"Humbly beg your pardon. All in the line of duty. We're studying the body politic. Are you free on Sunday?"

I came up with a quick lie. "My father's coming to visit." My father's been dead for years, but he's good enough to serve as an excuse.

"Fine. We'll come back another time then. By then your mister and missus should be back. And maybe then you'll be a little more gentle and German." They chugged what was left of a bottle of brandy just to be on the safe side, but not without saying "With your permission" and "To your health" and "*Pupille*—little doll, apple of our eye," probably to show what well-bred specimens of humanity they are. I thought: Just come back and try it, and I'll chop off something in your sleep. Not your head, but something you value much more. That'll put an end to your funny business.

I saw the whole lousy crew pull up in their motorcar. It was pretty early in the morning, and the first snow was falling. I don't know how the snow wasn't ashamed to fall on a day like that. But maybe it was ashamed and we just didn't notice. They were pointing their guns all over the place, at the buildings and the people in the street. The ground didn't open and swallow them up. Not yet, anyway. Give it some time. I know that for sure. But either way it really gave me the willies. Like most people around here. They say they're only after the Jews and political ones for now. But they won't stop at that. I don't know why I know that. My Mister and Missus, in any case, have up and left, and I'm stuck here with their money. It's just too crazy, it can't possibly end well. The two Gestapo men didn't even ask me about money, come to think of it.

I'm guessing they're dumb as the night is dark. And that'll be their downfall. People with badges, who sway their hips and gawk like turkey-cocks, can only be morons. That's our best hope. Below us, on the fourth floor, the woman with the little boy stopped and approached me on the stairs. "Are you going up to Hradschin Castle to greet the Führer? I'm going with Karli. An opportunity like this doesn't come twice in a lifetime."

"Yeah, yeah, I know," I said, "for Karli, that…"—and I wanted to say: that rotten knock-kneed milksop, but I said— "that bright little child of yours. But I've got spring-cleaning to do." I couldn't get myself to say "unfortunately."

"That they keep you busy with that on such a festive day," she says. She doesn't know that my Mister and Missus are long gone. You have to be careful with her.

"It's been planned for weeks," I say, "and I can't very well put it off now. You know how it is."

She doesn't know shit. But if you want to cut somebody off, you say: You know how it is. Of course I could have put on my new green polka-dot dress and gone up to Hradčany Castle. Maybe some guy would've approached me, and I would have snapped right back at him: "Where are your manners!" After all, I'm not a whore. Especially not for those guys, 'cause it's going to be nothing but Germans up there. And the worst sort. Not the kind like our Mister. Our Missus was actually Jewish. It took me three years to realize it, and only because she said so herself; then I forgot all about it. My mother always said: The Jews, they're not human. But first of all, what didn't she say; and second, she once had an affair with a Jew before he dumped her. That was before my father was around, and I know it from Uncle Peter. My father died not long afterwards. So he, too, dumped her in a way. A manure cart fell on top of him. I asked her once:

"Would you rather the dung cart had fallen on the Jew? Would that have made him a saint?" She smacked me one and called me a dirty little turd, which only goes to show that her head was full of crap.

Joška arrived today, from Šumperk. Her vulcanized-fiber suitcase had burst open and she tied it together with a piece of clothes line. I took a taxi from the station, to show her right off the bat who I am. I'd never splurged on one before. I probably gave too big of a tip, 'cause the driver said, "Thank you, ladies," and carried the broken suitcase to the door. Joška looked at me as if I were some kind of lunatic. "You're right," I said, "but I'm entitled." The lift was broken so we dragged the suitcase by the clothes line, all the way up to the sixth floor. The dame with the pathetic God-have-mercy son was standing in the doorway on the fourth floor, gaping.

"A pity you missed it."

"What?"

"What do you mean, what? The Führer, obviously."

All I said was: "The things I've missed in my life, you can't imagine." We continued lugging, and Joška asked, "Who on earth was that?" But we were already at the door, so all I said was, "A vicious cow," and dragged Joška into the apartment. "This is the Mister's room. But you'll sleep in the Missus's room. Here's the balcony. Check out the view. When you're down below there's a giant cemetery staring right at you, but from up here it looks like a garden. Makes you feel like the Good Lord himself, up so high that the whole shitty world seems like sheer splendor. The cemetery's huge, but you don't even notice there are dead people in it. And anyway, there's dead people in the ground all over. Way over there you can even see forests off in the distance. And to the left—you have to look down—that's Hradčany Castle. Yes, down there; we're higher up, so we have a bird's eye view. There's nowhere else like it in the entire city. Let me go make some coffee, then we'll unpack."

"And when are the master and mistress coming back?"

"Probably never. Don't worry about it, and keep your mouth shut. I'm in charge here now. You'll be sleeping in the Missus's room. I've got the Mister's bed. You have a fantastic sleeper ottoman, a wardrobe, table, chair, dresser and rugs—like a princess. Bet you never dreamed that your big sis could put you up like this, huh? Just look at what you're wearing! Grab a dress from the wardrobe and something for underneath from the dresser. She had a figure almost like yours."

"What do you mean, had?"

"She's probably still got it. But not here."

"Is that allowed? I mean the thing with the dresses and underwear?"

"Actually, it's not allowed. But I'm allowed. And so you're allowed too. You wouldn't believe how things are changing. If it weren't the way it were, it wouldn't be half bad. But the way it is, it makes my stomach churn. So get undressed and make yourself comfy. I bought a plum cake to go with the coffee. If I'd baked it myself it would have been better. But if you're rich you have to take it easy and try to be content."

"What, are you rich? Are you ill?"

"Not a trace, of one or the other. But I take it easy now, like the rich folks. They take it easy even if there's nothing the matter with them. Our sort has to learn that kind of thing. It's sweltering and they put on a cardigan. That's what they call refined. When our Missus came back from the theater and I asked her, 'So how was it?' she always answered: 'Nothing special.' People like us are happy if they can go to the pictures and cry over rich people falling in and out of love. But if you're refined you say, 'Nothing special.' If you can't get into the habit of that, you'll never amount to much in this world. Say you go out with some fellow and he blows his whole week's wages on one evening, including petty cash, and he asks you, 'Did you have a good time?' You have to answer: 'Nice enough, but not all that special.' Even if he roughs you up like a prizefighter in bed, you still have to say: 'Nothing special.'"

"How do you know all that?"

"Experience, my dear, experience. I've acted like an ordinary girl long enough, with my 'terrific, splendid, wonderful.' The Pyramids of Egypt? Nothing special. Here's the plum cake. I like to sprinkle grated almonds and minced lemon peel on mine. But what can you expect from people nowadays in exchange for your hard-earned money? First they leave out the lemon peel, then the grated almonds, then the plums, and eventually the flour. If they had it their way, they'd sell you baked air. I've finally found a decent coffee again with roasted chicory in it. My Mister and Missus always wanted pure bean coffee. They must have wanted to poison themselves."

Sleep, sleep in, as long as you want, stretch your arms and legs as far as they reach. Leave the clock alone if it stops. We don't need hours or time. It's all the same if we have breakfast at ten or eleven or twelve or twelve-thirty. The telephone's there still but doesn't ring, 'cause no one calls anymore. The doorbell hardly rings now either. Who would come? The things here are all in retirement. Let the dust gather, who cares. They belong to me now and the way you can tell is that I decide when to dust them. I'm in command now.

The reason I had Joška come was to have someone to boss around. It's hard to command when you're all alone. Do this, do that, and while you're at it that too. "You're worse than a mistress," says Joška. "Don't forget: You've never lived like this before, so free and easy," I say, "you can run around all day in your underwear. It's paradise." And she makes the most of it. The maintenance man came yesterday to do something on the water pipes, and the way she pranced around him was disgraceful. He took three times as long as he needed. But I gave her a piece of my mind. "That's no way to carry on with someone from the building, you cow. Now you have to let him have his fun so you've got him wrapped around your finger. If you don't, he'll tell everyone you're a whore. You really could try to be a little more mature."

I bought a dozen jazz records to keep us entertained. I can't listen to the old ones anymore. "Classical music," the Mister used to call it. I don't even know what that means. But I do know music should be good. And music is only good if, first of all, it makes you weep, second, if it makes you die laughing, and third, if it gets your legs and arms, your bosom and rear end moving and whirls you through the room like a maniac. The classical stuff just puts you to sleep. I love to watch when Joška dances like a savage to the gramophone. She says she learned it from the lady-help where she worked. Swinging around with your legs splayed, grimacing all the time, and making sure it all jiggles to your best advantage. I nearly die laughing. But then I give her a good smack in the face. A veritable Sodom and Gomorrah. "But it's the end of the world anyway," says Joška in her defense. The lady-help was a refined kind of girl, she could have gone to college. And she said, "If the world's about to end, you can do whatever strikes your fancy."

II

This afternoon at Wenceslas Square, one of the invaders in uniform suddenly stopped right in front of me. He saluted, clicked his heels with a bang, and said: "Excuse me, madam, may I humbly ask if you perchance have a command of the German language?" No one ever approached me so politely, and never with so many words. So I answer, even though he's one of the invaders: "You mean if I speak German? Yes, I do, if there's no way around it."

"In that case, may I respectfully request your counsel?"

"Request all you want, as long as it's respectful."

"I humbly beg you not to misunderstand me. But I'd like to buy some ladies' undergarments to send back home, to Chemnitz, I mean, and wanted to ask, if I may, where I could purchase them at a reasonable price."

I felt a little giddy from all the "humblys" and "respectful-lys" and "may I's." When somebody's that polite, you have to wonder why. And he was an invader on top of it all. Which is why I wanted to get rid of him, fast, so I said: "Right around the corner, at Ohrenstein and Koppelmann's. You can find all sizes and colors there, for a beanpole or an elephant."

"Many thanks for the useful particulars," he says. "But may I hazard a second request? If madam would have just a few moments to assist me in making my selections. I don't know much about these things, and frankly I'd be too bashful on my own."

Is this some newfangled way of picking up girls, I wonder. But no, the man really did look helpless and anxious. Kind of strange, if you think about it. A soldier, who's supposed to kill people when the time comes. But he gets all embarrassed when he has to buy women's underwear. So I tell myself: Go along, what could possibly go wrong, he spoke in such an educated way, and I can always tell him off if I have to.

"All right, what kind of figure does the lady have?"

"Oh, if you'll permit me to say so, almost like you, madam, which is why I took the liberty of addressing you."

His speech is so inflated, I think to myself, but I have to admit I like it. "Is it for your wife?" I ask, and bite my tongue as soon as I say it. What business is it of mine if it's for his wife or some other girl?

"Yes, ma'am! *Zu Befehl!*" he says.

"Did she give you orders?"

"No, ma'am, not at all. On the contrary. It's meant to be a surprise."

"Then why do you say it was an order—*zu Befehl?*"

"Oh, that's just a phrase, it doesn't mean anything, really. We Germans are always saying things like that. It just slips out involuntarily."

"But it's got to slip out from somewhere," I say. On the escalator at Ohrenstein and Koppelmann's he brushes my arm, but I saw right away it was unintentional, as far as a thing like that can be unintentional at all, because I don't really believe in chance or clumsiness. But he said, "Pardon me, I'm terribly sorry." "Why terribly?" I say, "normal sorry is enough." I was almost tempted to ask him: "Do you say 'I'm terribly sorry' before you shoot somebody?" I could imagine him doing it. Strange breed of people, these invaders. We go to the stall with ladies' undergarments and I help him choose. He likes all the stuff with transparent lace and pink ribbons and bows.

"Don't write to your wife and tell her you bought all this with me. She might get the wrong idea." At the same time I think to myself: You're a fine one! You've got the wrong idea yourself.

"Count on my discretion," he assures me, and says his name: Peter Something-or-Other, I didn't catch the whole thing, but Peter's enough, though I don't really know what that means: Enough for what? Then he goes and repeats his last name. His name is Gerstengranne—"barley awn"! I laugh a little, but then I think: It's better than "barley corn," and, anyway, what business is it of mine?

But it should be my business. Because he says we should meet next Sunday. Maybe for a walk in the *Baumgarten*, he's heard about our arboretum, and then (also a maybe) we can drop by a dance hall called the "Quelle," he's heard of that one too, supposedly they speak German there. So when and where can he hope to meet me on Sunday, he wants to know. I say "maybe" and "only if my sister comes along" and a few other things, 'cause you always have to kick up a fuss, but in the end we agreed to meet at the entrance to Stromovka, the arboretum, even though it's not the best season for walks. You walk through it and past Císařský mlýn, *Kaisermühle*, up to Bubeneč till you get to the "Quelle" dance hall. Now I've gone and done it. A rendezvous with an invader: I'll be a disgrace to everyone with character.

Sure enough, Joška turns up her nose when I tell her. But I bought her a new dress for her to wear on our outing. I bought two for myself, and anyway the ones that the Missus left behind have been on their hangers a little too long. But she can help herself to the costume jewelry, it's from Weblová's shop; the Missus probably left it behind because it looks too real. She's dolled up like a bride, but it's me who's the invader's type. I noticed that when we were picking out the underwear.

Joška comes along in the end, but something inside her balks. Gerstengranne is already waiting at the entrance to the arboretum, at the last tram stop. The buttons on his uniform are polished to perfection, he salutes with a crack of the heels, and is quick to answer Joška's grumpy *"Guten Tag"* with an "Ah, *Fräulein* has an excellent command of German."

I answer for Joška. "By nature we always speak Czech, but where we come from, near Znojmo, if you speak German there then you kind of do it like a *Vayner*."

"Humbly beg your pardon, what's *vejna*? I'm not too proficient in Slavic dialects."

"You know, the *Vayner*. Never heard of the imperial capital, *Vayn*?"

"Ah, *Wien*—Vienna. I see. Of course," he exclaims, "Viennese Blood, Vienna, Vienna You Alone, The Blue Danube, Wine, Woman and Song…"

"Now, now, let's not overdo it, and don't talk so loud. The folks here aren't too fond of that." And so we go for a walk. The trees have no idea yet what's going on in Prague. No need to be bashful in front of them. But maybe the trees have an inkling after all. What do we know about trees? Yesterday they came for the professor on the fifth floor. The Swastika lady with the loathsome little boy knew that he'd insulted the Führer. She was probably the one who reported him. He supposedly said that the Führer can kiss his… Colossal insult! But times are changing, I guess. You can say all you want about God these days, but Heaven forbid you should knock the Führer. They took the professor to the basement of Petschek Palace, I heard, and things are supposed to be pretty bad there. I think about this while we go for a stroll with Gerstengranne. I don't talk about it, that's for sure. Anyway, it's not his fault. Or is it? The trees and shrubs pretend that everything's like it always is. But what do they know. It's not spring yet. They've yet to awaken. There are still no butterflies and beetles. Who knows if there'll be any this year?

Gerstengranne is a corporal, but I call him sergeant 'cause it sounds a little more powerful. Gerstengranne doesn't walk, he marches. People stare at us with this look in their faces as if we were God knows what. Probably pretty stupid, what I've gotten myself into. But it's the kind of thing you blunder into, without really knowing how it happened. Before you know it, you're in the thick of it. Uncle Peter, the first one to do it with me—but why am I telling that story again, I've heard it enough—anyway, he said back then: You have to move with the times. And he was no dummy, Uncle Peter. Gerstengranne is called Peter too. Joška is walking a ways behind us, and seems to be sulking.

Luckily the arboretum is pretty empty. The only thing running around here is uniformed invaders or those in brown or black. The sergeant tries to explain the difference to me, but I'm not listening. I ask him about his wife instead, and if he has kids. But he's not listening to me either. Which is fine with me. What business is it of mine? We pass the old *Kaisermühle* and he asks: "Why do they call it that?"

"Probably because some Kaiser stopped there to eat once, or because the owner's name is Kaiser. Anyhow, they always eat *Olmützer Quargel* here now, that and coffee to go along with it."

"May I humbly ask what the word *Quargel* means?"

And these people want to conquer the world? "It's a kind of stinky cheese from the town of Olomouc, best when it gets a little runny."

"I see," he says, pensively. Then he adds: "The Kaisers, we've done away with them too."

The sign above the garden entrance to the "Quelle" has been repainted. The previous name, in Czech, "U Pramene," has been painted over and it now says "Zur Quelle." Could be worse, I suppose. Besides, they always got drunk here in German anyway. I never used to come here, but only because nobody brought me. I wouldn't treat myself alone. And anxiously waiting for someone to approach me and foot the bill, that wouldn't be my style. Of course, my pocketbook's full now, and I could order two portions of roast goose if I wanted to. I've also got a Gerstengranne taking me out. Unto every one that hath shall be given. Surely it won't last long. But a guy like this, who's finally away from his wife, he needs a pleasant change for one thing, and also a girl he can show off in front of. In any case, it's definitely good to have some dough in your own pocket. That way you can set the pace a little. It's more fun to do it gradually. Not like with Uncle Peter, who wanted to go all the way right from the get-go. Joška told me in the tub today that he was the same with her. He's dead now, so at least it'll stay in the family.

The sergeant takes a table near the window, in the hall where the music is playing. Joška plays coy, and says she'd rather walk some more. She's furious with this Gerstengranne. Actually she just wants to go to the john, and she looks at me to see if I'll come along. Go on your own. You don't do everything else in pairs. "I'll keep a seat reserved for madam," the sergeant says with a bow. Joška disappears. But two other seats at the table are unoccupied, and sure enough, while she's gone, two of these guys in black uniforms and jackboots come and say, "May we, madam?" Here we go. They're friendly, anyway, these murderers. Maybe they haven't murdered anyone here yet, but it's better to call them murderers right from the start so you don't have to correct yourself later. The sergeant doesn't look too happy about this, but what can he do? The two men introduce themselves. "Huber."—"Flaschenknopf." A decent fellow is called Hruška or Havlíček, like our Uncle Peter. Maybe he wasn't too decent, but at least he was Czech. Joška comes back and the two jump up like jack-in-the-boxes, holler "Huber" and "Flaschenknopf" again, then bang their boot heels together. I can tell the musicians are Czech by what they're playing, because every now and then they weave in a few of our old folk songs and dances. The Germans sitting here don't even notice.

> Oh Kolín, oh Kolín,
> You lie in a plain so green,
> And there pours a darling fine,
> Pours me fair and lovely wine,
> My sweetheart only mine.

The waiter comes to take our order. Gerstengranne proposes: "Perhaps we'll start with coffee and *Napfkuchen*?" I don't know what he means by *Napfkuchen*. We don't have a cake by that name here. He begins to explain it to me. But I don't like to be confused when it comes to food, so I just say, "Bring me a doughnut." Joška is brazen and says, "For me a fancy sandwich first."

"But Joška, that's a whole meal."

"I don't care, I'm hungry."

"Please, be my guest," Gerstengranne is quick to respond, and suggests a small glass of beer to go along with it.

"No, a large Pilsner," says Joška, and the sergeant resigns himself to his fate. He orders a Smichover for himself, takes a big gulp, leaving a foamy white mustache on his upper lip, and comments: "Boy, these Bohemian beers sure pack a punch."

Huber, one of the men in black, claims that Löwenbräu is much more drinkable. Flaschenknopf prefers Pschorr. Gerstengranne's for Pilsner, and Bohemian beers in general. He's tried them all since the invasion. "Well, in that case the Sudeten German ones," says Flaschenknopf, and mentions Leitmeritzer Bürgerbräu. "I don't know Leitmeritzer," Gerstengranne answers, "but I do know Gross-Popowitzer Bock."

"That's a Czech beer," explains Flaschenknopf, adding: "But what do the Saxons know about beer?"

"Nothing, that's what," Huber chimes in, "but they know how to make a weak coffee."

The atmosphere is tense. And when Gerstengranne makes an innocent remark: "In Chemnitz we like wheat beer with a dash of syrup," the two in black laugh so hard that the table starts to shake, and in the end a good-humored Gerstengranne even laughs along with them. And since the musicians are now playing "Tales from the Vienna Woods," things relax a little. The waiter brings Joška's open-faced sandwich, with ham, Hungarian salami, Swiss cheese, a deviled egg, a sardine and a dollop of Liptauer cheese spread, from which a mustard pickle protrudes between two sprigs of parsley and two capers. "A fine meal," says Gerstengranne. "Meal?" inquires Joška, "I'd call it a snack, 'cause later I'm gonna have roast beef in onions and gravy." At which point Gerstengranne falls silent, and the two in black order sandwiches like Joška's.

Flaschenknopf, it seems, wants to enjoy this sandwich to the fullest, because he gets up from his chair and—treading heavily in his jackboots, though not without a spring in his step and glancing in all directions—goes over to the musicians.

"Horst Wessel Song," he orders in a raspy voice.

"Come again?" the first violinist asks.

"Horst Wessel Song," squeals Flaschenknopf.

"I'm afraid it's not in our repertoire."

"What?!?" hollers Flaschenknopf, foaming at the mouth. He wrenches the fiddle from the violinist's hand and smashes it over his skull so hard that the wood cracks into pieces, and all that's left in his clenched fist is the neck of the violin, its splintered belly dangling from it on catgut strings. Jiminy crickets, I think, this is going to get ugly. And it did, indeed. Because it's Joška who gets up this time. She drops her fork and knife on the remainder of her open-faced sandwich, goes up to Flaschenknopf and nails him right in the kisser, so hard that he reels backward, and I can tell by the quality of her punch that she must have worked like a horse these years. Plucky girl, I think to myself. Someone in a corner applauds.

But Flaschenknopf's out of his mind now, and he jumps at Joška with his fists cocked. But Gerstengranne comes between them with a chair, shouting: "That's no way to treat a young lady." Flaschenknopf: "Lady? You mean whore!" whereupon Gerstengranne lets the chair fly, the seat of it whizzing right down on his head, while Joška lands a well-placed kick right between his legs; he hisses like a rattlesnake and falls back on the bandstand, hitting the nape of his neck on the edge, enough to finish him off, so thoroughly that no one knows if he's still alive or, hopefully, has croaked on the spot. Huber gets involved at this point, but not to assist his pal Flaschenknopf. He snarls at Gerstengranne: "You're fraternizing with enemies of the Reich." And at that moment two cops with pistols and armbands enter from the adjoining room, yell at everyone, and arrest whatever they can get their hands on. Gerstengranne, Joška and the violinist are rounded up, along with me, of course, and Huber who's the key witness, as well as four others who foolishly answered "yes" when asked, "Did you see it happen?" while a dozen people who'd been right in the middle of the action claimed they hadn't seen a thing, that everything was fine and dandy. Flaschenknopf, who was out cold, was carted away in an ambulance, while the rest of us had to wait for the "Green Anton," which is what they call police cars.

Suffice it to say, the outing was a memorable one. The first violinist, white as a sheet, keeps repeating, "*Já nic, já muzikant*"—I didn't do a thing, I'm just a musician. Joška bit her lip. "I really gave it him," she says, "right where it counts. He won't be forgetting that for a while." Joška's half-eaten sandwich is still lying on her plate, and the head waiter asks: "Who's going to pay for all this?" Gerstengranne is eager to pick up the tab for his and our part, but the police make a fuss 'cause they've already got him in handcuffs. Gerstengranne is a decent guy. So I pull out my wallet and cough up his share too, and he says, "I'll settle that later," to which Huber jeers: "If we let you, you traitor." Dear God in Heaven! These Germans. My Mister and Missus were also Germans. The only Germans worth putting up with are the ones who run from the Germans.

III

They've put away Joška. Me they let go, because top-boots Huber attested that I'd sat at the table motionless, eating my *Napfkuchen*. "Doughnuts," I say, 'cause I don't want to owe him anything. Still, they let me go. The violinist has to do three months in Pankrác prison, so he can learn the "Horst Wessel Song" there, they say. Gerstengranne, I was told, had to report to his commander, and no one knows what happened to him then. It's also unclear if his wife will ever get the pink underwear. I was lucky those cretins didn't question me about my present circumstances. When they asked about my profession, all I told them was "woman of private means." That made them more polite. If I'd told them "former maidservant" they probably would have caused me problems. The truth is exhausting. Anyway, I really am "private" now, 'cause I live off my own money. Not just any money, but cash, since I'm not about to put it in a savings account. That would look too suspicious. I'll stay in the apartment as long as it's paid for. And after that? Heaven only knows. If I try to sell off some of the stuff, they'll probably accuse me of stealing. But if I hold on to it, I don't know what to do with it. Once again, problems with the truth! Maybe the best thing would be to just leave it all behind, grab a suitcase and vanish one evening. But that would mean losing at least ten grand. I can't afford a loss like that, couldn't allow myself. The things they demand from people like me, it's really too much these days.

Maybe I could ask the friends of my Mister and Missus for advice. But first of all, most of them are Jewish and have got enough on their minds as it is, or, second, they've up and left already; and if they're Christian I have to be careful they don't end up turning me in. They say it's mostly the Jews they're after, and plenty of my Czech friends are perfectly fine with that. As far as they're concerned, all the Germans living here are Jews, even the ones who are Christians ten times over. They don't discriminate. And what about the invaders? Who really knows? My friend Ella from Chlum

Svaté Maří was about to marry a real Jew. He's pious, she said, and pious is good whether you're Jewish or not. She was even willing to do the Jewish thing herself. The Missus shook her head when Ella told her about it, but when she saw how persistent my friend was she eventually recommended a Jewish clergyman who might give her lessons. I said to her: "Ella, why are you doing this? What's gonna happen when you want to celebrate Christmas with a Christmas tree and all that jazz? The town you come from is a pilgrimage site."—"Makes no difference," she says, "I'll celebrate my Christmas and he'll celebrate his." She went to the Jewish temple every Friday, already in the afternoon. "Mass starts at five," she said, and the marriage was all set. Then all the trouble with the invaders starts and the husband-to-be says to Ella: "Listen, I've gotta get out of here. My boss is well-informed and advised me to clear out as fast as I can. He's leaving next week. He gave me money. Why don't you come with me."—"But where to?" asks Ella. "To America, of course. We can still make it."—"What?" cries Ella, "To America? Me? You want me to live with savages? A woman like me from Chlum Svaté Maří?" And so she let him go. But a few weeks later she came to me: "Hey, I feel something inside me and I don't know what to do." So I sent her to Paní Bulinová, who's experienced in those things. At first she said, "I'm retired, and I feel like puking when I see a woman's belly," but she took on Ella after all, and everything turned out fine. At first Ella said, "It's because I prayed to the

49

Holy Mother of God of Chlum Svaté Maří when I wanted to turn Jewish." But she still hasn't gotten over the loss of her fiancé, just like my mother hasn't gotten over hers, the one she had before my father, the guy I got slapped in the face for mentioning. But Ella, she says: "The Jews are no different from other people, I know that well enough." Of course she should know it. That Nazi floozy from the fourth floor, on the other hand, the one with the awful subhuman child, she told me not long ago in the hallway: "The most important thing is to get rid of all the Jews." So I asked her, "Did one of them ever do anything to you?"—"God forbid, I've never even talked to one. But everyone knows how awful they are." I said no more.

Our Missus was a Jewess. But she was a much better person than Director Proschetitzky, who might have gone to church every Sunday but locked up the sugar and the butter and the flour and the eggs and the coffee and even the paper napkins before she left, 'cause she took me and everyone else for thieves. She lugged around a big key chain on her belt, with at least twenty different keys, and all day long you heard nothing but the constant unlocking and locking of cabinets and drawers, until her husband finally poisoned himself with cyanide. I went to the Lichtenbergs' when it happened. That Proschetitzky woman wouldn't believe it at first that her husband would kill himself. And when they proved it to her through the autopsy, she told me afterwards: "He was always somewhat mentally disturbed."

I became furious and screamed at her: "Anyone living with you, Frau Proschetitzky, would have to be crazy not to kill himself." And then I left for good.

They let out Joška, just three weeks later, which really surprised me. But I nearly had a stroke when she brought the guy in the black uniform and jackboots with her, that Flaschenknopf fellow, the one she kicked in the groin at the "Quelle." I wasn't going to let them in at first, but then she said, "Marška, don't be silly. If it wasn't for him I'd still be in there. They would have sent me to a camp or something. He's not as bad as he looks."

"Yes, ma'am," he said, resuming the rigmarole where Joška left off, "it's true what she says. Had too much alcohol beforehand, which is why I've revised my original statements. Was all just a clumsy mishap. Humbly ask your forgiveness." And then he adds: "Fräulein Joška's energetic behavior very much impressed me and filled me with admiration."

So basically a kick in the groin is how a woman makes a good impression on these people. But that can't be everything. He must have made a strong impression on Joška too. She wouldn't have thrashed him like that otherwise. It seems to me now that the brawl was nothing but a declaration of love. She put such a spoke in his wheel that he couldn't shake the feeling and the smell of her, and told himself while convalescing: I've got to have her! then scouted her out with every trick in the book. And now she's grateful to him, of course, and thinks the world of him. I don't know what I should do or say. The bastard comes almost every day or evening. I hear the two of them going at it at night and feel all queasy in the loneliness of my bed. The worst thing, though, is the uncertainty. Because secrets are revealed in bed. Not long ago I told her: "Joška, don't you have any sense of honor?" And she came right back at me: "What do you want me to do? If I don't go with him, he'll get us into trouble. He knows who your mister and missus were, and where you've got your money from."—"What?" I scream, "You told him that too?"—"He had me over a barrel, and tormented me to the point that I felt like nothing mattered anymore."—"Did you tell him how much?"—"How much? You haven't even told me. But he's really nice, and always brings little presents for me."—"I'd rather you had a Czech sewer cleaner. I wish the earth would swallow me every time that creature on the fourth floor winks at me. I could murder her. And it's all because of you."—"You can't have everything the way you want. People get used to anything. Once learnt, never forgotten."—"Cut the goddamn proverbs. You can use them to justify murder. How do you know how many people this Flaschenknopf hasn't knocked off already."—"Oh, come on! He's the son of a teacher and his uncle's a pastor."—"Good God, a Protestant too. Those are the worst. If he were Jewish at least."—"Jewish? Were you dropped on your head as a baby, or what? It's his job to kill them. He always sings that song to me: When Jewish blood spurts from the knife, then all is twice as nice."

I gave her such a smack in the face it was all she could do to keep from falling. And she hissed at me: "Watch out you don't wind up in the clink yourself. It wouldn't be hard for me to arrange." At which point I became truly scared, and saw that our sisterly coexistence was over, that I had to fear her now like an enemy, that there'd be no taking it easy anymore, that she can crush me like a cockroach if she wants to. And I stammered: "I didn't mean it that way. What's the harm in smacking your little sister now and then." And I was happy all she said was: "Well then. You know where I stand. Just don't cause any problems."

I won't cause problems anymore, big or small. I don't say a thing to her, and just let it slide. I used to think that people should be like interlocking gears, where the one always keeps the other in check a little bit so you don't go rolling downhill out of control. Now I think: Let it roll. I'm just wondering how it's come to this. First the Mister and Missus went away and left me all their money and belongings. I'm not sure anymore if that was such a good thing. Then I found some more money. That probably wasn't a good thing either. Then I met Gerstengranne. That was the biggest misfortune of all. Why did all of this happen to me? Did he have to buy her the pink underwear and those things, in Prague of all places? And couldn't he have found someone else besides me? It would have all been fine if it weren't for Joška. But no, I had to have Joška here so I could flaunt it in front of her and boss her around. And now she's giving me orders.

That's the fate of people who want to lord it over others. There wouldn't have been a brawl at the "Quelle," and that scoundrel in top boots wouldn't be lounging around here either. Joška doesn't lift a finger, and always runs around all gussied up. I have to cook and clean, and am now my sister's servant on top of it. And whenever I protest she looks at me and I know exactly what she's thinking: "Shut up and be happy they don't come haul you away for questioning. You can thank me for that." The people in the building look away when I pass them, 'cause of course they see that guy coming and going. Only the lady on the fourth floor acts friendly, which makes me want to scream.

And I have to fork over cash too. He doesn't even take her out. She takes him out. I've already shelled out a big part of the money. I have to hide what's still left of it. Every night I ponder for hours where the safest place would be. Not long ago I came up with the idea of burying it in some grave at the cemetery. I even went there, and bought a bouquet of red gladiolas so I wouldn't attract too much attention, and walked around for ages till I found a really old, untended grave that no one was ever likely to visit. Cemetery VIII, Section 6, Number 176. One of the arms of the wooden cross was broken off. I laid down the gladiolas there. The grave was really secluded, tucked away behind lilac bushes. I knelt down and was about to start digging with a cake server when, sure enough, a caretaker comes and says, "I'm really glad you want to plant something and that someone is taking care of these abandoned graves. I assume it's a relative of yours? Can I help you?"—"No," I say, "thank you. I just came to check on things and wanted to pray a little." And I really did pray for this unknown dead person, underground and long forgotten. Then I packed up my boodle and went back home. Maybe, when all is said and done, the only reason I had the money and all the anxiety that went along with it was just so that some unknown dead person with a broken cross would get prayed for. What a life!

How can it be that something completely sickens you and still you guard it like a treasure? My wages never sickened me. The thing is, I used to work for them. But the money that fell in my lap has something alien about it. Yet still I protect it and coddle it, always wrapping it up like a baby in swaddling clothes. Why did I ever have Joška come? I'm much too kind. She's young and pretty and dissolute. She carries around her capital with her. She can always pick up someone. What she doesn't know is that her black-clad Flaschenknopf is chasing after me too. Not long ago, when I was hanging the freshly laundered curtains, he came up from behind and shook the ladder until I came tumbling down into his arms. It was awful, but not unpleasant. Ever since then, it's been something different each day. And it always ends up with me being alone with him. It was never like that before. Then, when Joška comes, they go at it like always, they hole themselves up, and I think she squeals extra loud just to get on my nerves.

Today at lunchtime I got back from shopping and noticed that something wasn't right. I always put the folded laundry in the dresser in a very precise and specific manner, a way that only I know, because I thought of it myself. The pressed handkerchiefs, for example, are always staggered, their corners just touching the hem of the underskirts. It's not about order, it's so I can find out right away if someone's been messing with my things. Everything was well-ordered today, but now the corners aren't right. Something was wrong with the other drawers too. I always put a little powder on the brass knobs, but today it was like they were polished. Obviously it was Joška, she was after my money. She was in my wardrobe too. I measured the rod with a tape measure and marked it off with a pencil, and I always put the hangers at an equal distance from each other. No trace of that now. Same with the couch cushions. The mattresses weren't perfectly aligned, the cushions were not in a row, and in the middle, where I always punch it with my fist to make it look a little fluffier, it was flat.

Of course she didn't find a thing. 'Cause I always carry the remaining bills in two pouches on my thighs, left and right, underneath my skirt. My rear end is wide enough, and this way no one will notice. Whenever I have to get undressed, I do it in such a way that I always keep an eye on the two money pouches. Administering an estate is a real pain. With a magpie like Joška, there's no safe hiding place in any apartment. Anyway, they don't build apartments for people who've always got something to hide from each other, even though most people probably do.

The rent is due again soon. Joška, of course, says, "Don't worry about it. Flash—that's what she calls Flaschenknopf—can straighten out that kind of thing, no problem. With him around, there's no need to pay rent. And Herzig, the building owner, is a Yid anyway; they're coming for him tonight."

"How do you know that?"

"Ha-ha, I know more than you think, 'cause what I know doesn't come from using my head. I learn things my own way. I know, for example, that the rent is due, and I told Flash I want to stay here. You don't plan on leaving, do you?"

"But I could have paid the rent! And Herzig might not have even asked."

"What, you want to throw our money in his greedy maw? And if I hadn't told Flash, the woman on the fourth floor would have. She knows him, and has to pay rent too."

She says "our money," cool as a cucumber. And I'm fretting about Herzig, who of course is none of my business. But when suddenly you share the blame for something without having done anything, that gives a decent person the creeps. And I do share the blame. Joška is my flesh and blood, and she lives with me, and we have the same mother. Maybe not the same father, but that's not really so important. It's the mother that counts. And mine told me: "Keep an eye on her. She'll stop at nothing, and someday she'll get herself into a real pickle." It was my duty, in other words, to keep her out of this pickle, especially since it was me that had her come here in the first place. Beating up Flaschenknopf and going to prison for it, that wouldn't be so bad. I was even a little proud of her. But flirting and sharing her bed with him, now that's a real disgrace. And now this on top of it, and her being after my money, and even calling it "our money"—that really takes the cake. Yesterday Flash says to me, before going up to the bedroom with Joška: "You mind polishing up my boots a little in the meantime?" In the meantime! As if I were his servant girl! But what do I do? I really do go and polish his boots, buff them till they shine, I really do act like a servant girl. When somebody gives me orders like that, I'm what people call hypnotized. But this fellow? Not so much as a thank-you once his "in the meantime" is over. What will it all come to? You never know what's going to happen to you, but I shouldn't let it get to that point. Which is true for Joška and true for me. No, it really shouldn't go that far.

I rang the bell downstairs at Herzigs' and his wife opened the door for me. They don't have a maidservant anymore. His wife gave me a terrified look, and when I ask if I can maybe speak to Herr Herzig, she looks even more terrified and asks, "How come?" All I can think of is, "Because of the rent," and this calmed her down a little. She leads me through the hall, past a couple of suitcases into the parlor, and says to her husband: "It's Marška from the sixth floor, she's here because of the rent."

Herr Herzig looks up, and even smiles a little. "Oh, don't lose any sleep on account of the rent. There's time, plenty of time."

Suddenly it's silent. I don't dare speak up. I don't want to kill his friendly smile. He's an older man, around fifty, and whenever you run into him he always asks how everything's going, if everything's all right in the apartment, and if there's anything you need. He was always a kind landlord. It wrings my heart to tell him, but I can't just leave now and let things run their course. So I finally break the silence: "Herr Herzig, don't be angry with me. It's not about the rent at all."

"Is that so. So what's on your mind then?"

"It's because I wanted to warn you, so nothing bad happens to you."

"What could possibly happen to me?" he asks, and I can see he knows what I want to say, so he adds: "I haven't done anything against the law."

"Of course not. But I heard they're coming for you tonight."

"And how can you know that for sure? Who told you that?"

I don't answer. Frau Herzig is sitting on the couch with her head resting in her hand, and Herr Herzig paces the room. His face has gone red and it seems like he's angry.

"Herr Landlord," I say, "I beg you, don't be angry at me. And don't ask me too many questions. Because whatever you ask me, I can't answer it in this lifetime. I can only say that I know it for sure, and that I'm scared for you and the missus. My Mister and Missus left a long time ago. Please listen to me, and don't wait around too long."

Silence once again, and I look around the room and wonder what will happen to the silver box and the onion-pattern dishes behind the glazed sideboard, and I think that poor Frau Herzig is thinking the same thing as me. But then he says: "You're just trying to scare us, Fräulein. You're having gloomy thoughts."

"Very gloomy, Herr Herzig, believe me. But they're more than thoughts. I implore you: Leave everything behind and make sure you get out of here today before nightfall. Tomorrow morning will probably be too late. Don't wait, don't do that to me."

"Why you? What does any of this have to do with you? Or do you have an inside line or something?"

"I have nothing and everything to do with it. The truth is I'm asking you for your own sake, for my sake too, and also for the sake of my sister. You won't understand all that, and I can't explain it to you, not in all eternity, amen. But for the love of God: Get out of here, now. I can't stay here any longer."

"But how do you expect us to do that? Even if I wanted to leave, we don't have passports, and no exit permits. Where are we supposed to go?"

"Anywhere, Herr Herzig, anywhere. Just don't stay here. I'm being straight with you. There are moments, Herr

Herzig, when you shouldn't ask questions and shouldn't wait around. There's just one door and you have to pass through it. I say that to you and to myself. The things that are right are only worth something if it's true for you as well as for the others. I had to come see you. I'd never be able to forgive myself otherwise. For Heaven's sake, can't you see how desperate I am?"

"You're a little bit hysterical, it's no wonder in times like these. Calm down, please. It won't cost us our heads, or yours for that matter. Why should anything happen to you? Rest assured, we won't tell anyone that you were here. And I repeat: I've never done anything against the law in my entire life. I paid my taxes, was an officer in the Great War, even a liaison officer with a German division, and was recommended for the Iron Cross. I didn't get it, unfortunately. The war was just coming to an end. But I got the big silver one, have a look over here, in the glass cabinet."

"Herr Landlord, I don't think you understand me. These fellows who come to take people away at night, they have no respect for anything, there's nothing you could show them, even if you had ten Iron Crosses. I know. There's nothing you can do or say to convince them. Not even with money. Because they'll take it anyway. I only know one thing: If you don't pack the bare necessities and disappear with the missus before nightfall, you'll bring misfortune to you and your wife and all of us."

"Now I'm really getting impatient. Why 'all of us'? Who do you mean, 'all of us'? You can't make us responsible for something that happens to you, assuming it would happen at all, which I highly doubt."

"Herr Herzig, I beg you, you wouldn't believe how much we're responsible for, how much is our fault, what we've done and what we've neglected. I know what I'm talking about. I won't talk about it though. It would take me until the day after tomorrow. And your time is precious. The day after tomorrow you might not be there to listen to me anymore. For the last time: I beseech you—on my knees. Holy Mother of God, I've tried. I told you and I told myself. Maybe the only reason I came was to tell myself. Don't wait any longer. If you need help packing, I'm there."

"That's very kind of you," Herr Herzig says, "but I really don't need anyone's help. For anything at all."

"Excuse the disturbance. I meant well." And with that I went.

IV

The elevator's not working again and, climbing the stairs from the Herzigs', my legs are like blocks of cement, crashing down on each step. I'm only in my early thirties, but the last months have weighed on me like decades. Crawling up the stairs, I'm mortified when it occurs to me that I didn't bring the money pouches with me; I stuck them in the old

Russian samovar while changing my clothes and forgot them there when I went down to the landlord. Hopefully those two were busy while I was gone. But the thought that they might have been snooping around doesn't make my legs any lighter. I want to get up there as fast as I can. They say that fear makes you run, but maybe fear knows what happened already, so that now there's no reason to strain myself. I climb the stairs slowly, puffing and panting, step by step, boom, boom, boom. My steps ring out like cannon shots at a military funeral. Nobody is in the stairwell. There's a niche with a plaster vase in it on every landing. I stop a few seconds at each one. I do it so the vases have some kind of purpose. I'm at the fifth one already. Our door is next to the sixth.

There's not a sound from Joška's room. Why are the two of them so quiet? They're way too quiet. I go to my room and lift the copper crown from the samovar, then the sieve inside. Empty. Nothing left there. Joška! No answer. Her door is unlocked. They're gone.

It's not about the money. When you get right down to it, I'm even kind of happy that it's gone. It'll keep on eating away like acid, wherever it goes. My Mister even said once that all the money in the world is nothing but the interest on Judas's thirty pieces of silver. They're still in circulation and are multiplying, and Jesus is still being bartered away. Of course in that case he had no good reason to slip the poison in my hand in the first place.

I'll stay here and wait. For what? I stand at the door of the apartment and listen for sounds from the floors below. What kind of sounds? It's already late in the afternoon, but it gets dark pretty late now. From the stairwell it sounds like the house is deserted. Not many people go out now. A few people come home around six. I know exactly which floors they live on, and sometimes I hear them talking at their doors. That was Herr Sichrovsky, the druggist. He said something to his wife. You used to hear them yelling and fighting all the time. Now you almost only hear them whisper. It's not a good sign, I think, when people start to whisper. I stand and I stand and I always know who's coming, I can tell which floor by the sound of the bell. And so the hours pass. Hours and hours. I can hear from way down below as the janitor's wife goes to lock the front door. Paní Vladislavská. She doesn't quarrel with her husband anymore either. The light goes out in the stairwell. It's pitch-dark. So it must be past ten o'clock. That's how long I've been standing at the door. But only now does my vigil begin. I leave the door open a crack to hear better. Moonlight falls through the stairwell window, right onto our plaster vase in its niche. It grins like a face. Maybe it is one, and only transforms into a vase in the daytime. Who knows what things really are? No one can really say what humans are either. Eleven o'clock. I hear the church bell ring at the nearby cemetery. It's odd enough that it has a clock at all, because isn't that where time stops? But maybe it's so the dead will know how long they have to wait till resurrection.

What a racket that'll make. And all the waiting and being dead will have been for nothing anyway, because it's then that the actual Judgment comes.

The front door rings. I know this ringing well. You can't hear it in the apartments, but it echoes through the stairwell. The bell really booms today. I hear the janitor's wife, too, going to unlock the door. She drags her old slippers slowly across the tiled floor. When her husband goes to open the door, you hear the firm steps of shoe-shod feet. She talks to some people at the door. There are at least four voices, three male ones and the voice of Paní Vladislavská. I can't understand them, but I know what's happening.

The electric light goes on in the stairwell. I hear men's footsteps and an argument in the stairwell. And now they ring at Herzigs'. They ring three times and knock on the door. It must be open now, because I hear the voice of Herr Herzig clearly. And I hear Frau Herzig sobbing. I can even understand what Herr Herzig says. "I haven't done anything against the law." Or I think I understand, because I know he'll say it. But his objections and protestations about the Iron Cross and the Great Silver Medal for Bravery are drowned out by the three other male voices, which aren't even human voices at all, they're not even animal voices, because even wolves have some kind of justice. Who knows what kind of beings they are.

It's quiet now for a while. They probably went into Herzigs' apartment and he's getting dressed and packing some things. Jesus, Mary and Joseph, I told him and he wouldn't believe me! They come back out again now. I hear Frau Herzig, her voice is loud but unintelligible. The men are swearing. Paní Vladislavská, who was waiting outside, unlocks the front door and locks it again. I hear her shuffling back in her slippers. Then the stairwell is dark and silent again.

That was the first part of my vigil. Now I have to wait till Joška gets back. And then I have to wait till this night of waiting comes to an end. So Joška wasn't making it up. She really did do it, the thing with the money and with Herr Herzig. I would have looked the other way with the money. Easy come, easy go. And who does money belong to anyway? I wait my way through, slowly, through the whole apartment, through the hallway, the three rooms and through the kitchen with all of its pots, pans, spoons, forks and knives. That was my life. I loved the old Italian knife-grinder, who always came at Christmastime and parked his grinder's cart outside the building. What's he going to live off of when everyone starts using Nirosta stainless-steel knives that you don't even need to sharpen? I love the old ones, with their long, curved blades and the marks left by the grindstone that make the edge sparkle and the tip disappear in an invisible world.

I lie down in the dark for a while and hear Joška at the door. She tries not to wake me, and has good reasons not to. She tiptoes into her room and doesn't even switch on the light. But still she can't suppress the urge to hum to herself very quietly. They came for Herzig and she's humming. Frau Herzig is downstairs crying. I hear it, even if I don't hear it. And Joška's humming. It's not about the money. One person steals from the next. She opens the door to the hallway now, 'cause she likes to have a little breeze. The waiting is almost over, until her breathing is heavy and even.

Our Master is a writer. I wonder if someday, in a foreign country, he'll imagine what went on inside me, why I became the way I am now, and why I have to do what I'm about to do. I wonder if he'll write it down the way I lived it, and everything that went through my mind while it happened? I wonder if he'll be on my side when they summon him as a witness at the Last Judgment? Maybe he'll come forward and swear: "I wasn't there when it happened, and yet I was there. I share the blame. I should have known better, because I was the one who gave her the money."

She starts to breathe more deeply now. She doesn't hear me. Even when she sleeps all she hears is herself. The knife's wavy handle is clenched securely in my fist. The moon caresses her neck. Jesus, Mary and Joseph!

THE DUCHESS OF ALBANERA

For Max Brod

WITH:

The bank clerk Wenzel Schaschek
The delicatessen-store owner Mader
His assistant Ferda
The janitress Paní Kralíková
The janitor Pan Kralík
Eleonor, the Duchess of Albanera
The museum director
The museum director's assistant
The museum guard Novotný
The pedestrian Walter Fürth
The bank director
The bank manager

THE BANK CLERK Wenzel Schaschek left the building of Union Bank on Na příkopě and—like every day after work—headed towards Havířská Street, passing the old Bohemian State Theater and entering Herr Mader's delicatessen store. Herr Mader gave his store that name to show that he didn't, or didn't merely, offer the usual run of comestibles for stilling a vulgar hunger but was adapted to more sophisticated tastes. He always had the best French sardines in stock, Dresden sausage appetizers, Lomnitz zwieback, Carlsbad wafers, Elbogen gingerbread, gray, large-grained Malossol caviar, and Strasbourg goose-liver pâté. And when they were in season, he'd also have a lobster or a pineapple. Whatever the case, the whole store smelled like saltwater fish, because Herr Mader was the only one in Prague who imported them back then. This was a business tradition. Grandfather Mader, whose sister had married a man from Mecklenburg, laid the foundations of the business by trading in dried cod, smoked eel, flounder, bloaters and kippers, peppered fish and pickled herring. And however much son and grandson skillfully expanded their business horizons with a selection of sausages and cold cuts, with quality cheeses and wines *en primeur*, the true-to-life cod painted on the signboard by a valiant local artist was nothing less than a city landmark, which the Mader family clung to with religious atavism.

But Herr Mader the Third was adamantly opposed to being addressed as a mere fishmonger. He had even read Brillat-Savarin (in a Reclam edition), and the always well-endowed wheel of Swiss cheese displayed a little plaque bearing the gilt inscription: "A dinner which ends without cheese is like a woman with only one eye."

Herr Schaschek entered this delicatessen, turned to Ferda, the white-aproned assistant standing behind the counter, and said: "Ham." At this point it should be noted that the celebrated Prague ham was normally bought at the pork butcher's. But, first of all, Herr Schaschek was a special person, as this report endeavors to show; second, Herr Mader stocked a special kind of ham, chimney-smoked just for him by butcher Sykora in Křivoklát and not available anywhere else; third, Herr Schaschek's relation to Herr Mader's store was one of character-defining continuity. Which is why he just said: "Ham."

At that, the assistant Ferda looked first at Herr Schaschek, then at his boss, Herr Mader, every bit astonished, repeated in a highly troubled and questioning tone, "Ham?" then added: "Beg your pardon, sir, but you just had ham yesterday, shouldn't it be Hungarian salami today?"

"No, ham," declared Schaschek with sulky defiance. "I'm a free man, after all." Following this conjecture, which had something menacing about it thanks to the insertion of the words "after all," the assistant Ferda, mute and swallowing his disbelief, grabbed the very long carving knife, made slender from years of sharpening but still razor-sharp, cut into the ham that was held in place by a metal clamp on the chopping board, and carefully shaved off six thin slices with a rose-quartz gleam and the delicate, pervading scent of freshly cured meat, laid them terrace-fashion on parchment paper, weighed them on the well-tared brass scale (which wasn't really necessary, since Ferda had an infallible eye for fifteen dekagrams of ham, but was nonetheless part of the ceremony), then wrapped it all in brown packing paper, and said with anguish in his voice, "Thirty-six hellers, please."

For those who haven't yet noticed, these details should make apparent that this whole procedure is taking place in the days of the old Austrian monarchy, a golden era, inasmuch as a kilogram of ham still cost two crowns and forty hellers—or, for the more conservative-minded, who viewed the currency transition from florins to crowns as a Catilinarian craze for novelty and an assault on the very existence of the empire (and probably weren't wrong about it): one florin and twenty kreutzers. Schaschek, still a boy at the time of the currency reform, had asked his father back then, "Why do you always call twenty hellers a six-kreutzer?" He was given the answer: "A florin has always been sixty kreutzers, ever since the world began. A tenth of that is six kreutzers, hence a six-kreutzer. All this fiddle-faddle nowadays has turned a florin into two crowns or two hundred hellers, a tenth of which, that is to say twenty hellers, is a six-kreutzer, got it?"

But to understand the real significance of this delicatessen scene and the confusion, if not to say consternation, of the assistant and his boss, one needs to know that Herr Wenzel Schaschek was in the habit of entering Herr Mader's store at the same time every day of the week, ordering fifteen dekagrams of Hungarian salami on Monday, Wednesday and Friday, and fifteen dekagrams of ham on Tuesday, Thursday and Saturday, always in that sequence, and never anything else. The day in question was Wednesday, hence salami day, whose sudden transformation into ham day was tantamount to an elementary catastrophe for those involved. Since the Mader family's charwoman was related by marriage to Schaschek's janitress, Herr Mader knew that Schaschek was wont to take his supper at "Zum Prinzen" restaurant. The bachelor's morning coffee was prepared on a spirit burner.

Schaschek had slipped the wrapped-up ham in his coat pocket, whence he heard that satisfied murmur he was used to hearing whenever he purchased ham, and which went something like this: "Praise God, the penultimate station on the path of my blessed transformation has been reached. I'm going to taste good." "Don't give yourself airs," Schaschek barked at the ham. Hungarian salami was more reserved, for the raw materials used to make it were processed into a chaotic jumble, allowing only limited possibilities of expression. Schaschek now turned his steps towards Rytířská Street to procure a freshly pickled cucumber, not too big, not too small, from one of the market women there, a pickle it was better not to store in your coat pocket, since the pickle woman had wrapped it up in newspaper, which back then wasn't as sickening as it would be later on. The newsprint, at any rate, absorbed the salty-sour juice, which smelled like dill and allspice, and which formed the pickle's element of existence; and since this in itself rather tasty brine would have made Schaschek's coat pocket wet, he decided to keep the pickle in his hand. In doing so his gaze scanned one of the newspaper headlines, which ran: "Still No Trace of the Duchess of Albanera."

"Good thing," said Schaschek contentedly. The pickle, however, which he carried in front of him vertically, held aloft by three fingers, dripped milky-opal tears. "Don't cry like an imbecile," said Schaschek, "the Duchess is just fine." The pickle did in fact take its master's words to heart and soon found solace, while its bearer turned onto Karlova Street and presently, at said place, reached the entrance of his building, where he lived on the second floor facing the courtyard, in a room with a kitchenette. He practically never used the latter, least of all the stove. The kitchen, for all intents and purposes, served as his storage room.

The building itself was a venerable one, well-nigh historic. A variety of important individuals had supposedly lived there, and Schaschek sometimes felt a shudder of world historical proportions when, crossing the courtyard by way of the access balcony (called *Pawlatsche* in Prague, which according to folk etymology, he well knew, is derived from *parvula loggia*), he walked to the lavatory, which was shared by the other tenants on his floor, and in doing so thought that perhaps Cola di Rienzo or maybe even the great Petrarch himself had sat on the ancient, grayish-black oaken toilet seat, which with time had become nearly petrified. The oak board serving as a seat creaked a few times in the stony grooves it was sunk in on both sides. The rest of the oak tree stood in the form of a coffer up on Castle Hill, the Hradschin, in which was kept the Letter of Majesty reluctantly signed by melancholic Emperor Rudolf I, thereby granting the Bohemian Protestants all kinds of different rights. This coffer had the same woodgrain pattern, the same cross-section through the annual rings as the seat on Schaschek's lavatory, Schaschek having noticed this secret correspondence once while viewing the Emperor's apartment. Perhaps the oak board creaked and groaned from a restrained sense of longing or stifled resentment.

Schaschek, still holding the pickle ceremoniously in front of him, ran into the janitor Kralík on the landing of the first floor, the husband of said relative of Mader's charwoman, a man who when asked in greeting "How are you?" would always reply with a slightly moaning singsong "*Táhneme to*," which basically meant, "Still trudging along," not unlike the "*Ey, ukhnem*" of the Volga boatman that was turned into a famous folk song. This time he didn't answer *"Táhneme to,"* though, but simply said, "Your window facing the *Pawlatsche* was´open, but my wife closed it for you. Because it rained at noon for one thing, Herr Schaschek, not to mention that someone could have climbed into your apartment and carried off something valuable."

"What do you mean, something valuable?" Schaschek asked, the pickle in his hand wobbling ever so slightly.

"Well, everyone's got something valuable, don't they," the janitor Kralík explained.

"Of course," said Schaschek, "many thanks." It didn't even cross his mind to ask what exactly gave Paní Kralíková the authority to use her master key and open his apartment to make sure everything's in order. It was none of her beeswax if he left his window open. But he was careful not to stir up a lawsuit. No one could win against the Kralíks. Not even the landlord, Herr Schimek, who descended from a family of comic actors, was able to win against them, when instead of the lock-out six-kreutzer customarily paid to Paní Kralíková for opening the front door after ten at night—Pan Kralík didn't open for anyone—he wanted to provide the tenants with their own keys to the building. Well, what do you know, the lock on the front door suddenly stopped working and the tenants had to ring Paní Kralíková to come open it. Installing a new lock on the oak-plank door from the era of Charles IV, with its Gothic wrought-iron ornamentation, would have been impracticable; a whole new front door would have had to be custom-made, which not only would have been costly but would have met with objections from the Office for Historical Preservation. "You see, Herr Schimek," Paní Kralíková had said, "what doesn't work just doesn't work."

So Schaschek, carrying his pickle, entered his living quarters without another word. Luckily he had stowed away all the things that mattered to him in his big, old armoire, to which there was only one key, and this he had in his pocket. The lock, made of engraved steel, had all kinds of springs and complicated, interlocking gears. Like opening a bank vault, one had to repeatedly twist the key back and forth using a certain magic formula before its double doors would open. This broad, heavy cabinet was from the Vienna of Maria Theresa's day, and was what you call an heirloom. Not that Schaschek had inherited it. Rather, he had bought it on a sudden extravagant impulse with his first monthly salary when he moved into this apartment after the death of his father. He had seen it at an antique dealer's, with a sign attached to it reading "heirloom."

"Who inherited it from whom?" asked Schaschek.

"I don't know," said the antique dealer, "but armoires like that are always heirlooms."

The cabinet had curved flanks, its wing doors swiveled in fluted pilasters, and the surfaces were elaborately inlaid with variously tinted woods. The hinges, which sometimes gave a disgruntled screech, Schaschek calmed with a little salad oil. This piece of furniture had weathered the Seven

Years' War, the French Revolution, the Bonaparte era, the Revolution of 1848, as well as the rest of the century with its telegraphs and railroads. "It'll survive Paní Kralíková, too," muttered Schaschek, who was irritated that he'd been so careless to not close the window.

Having turned on the light, closed the curtains and bolted the apartment door from inside, he freed the warty, greenish-yellow, sour pickle from its soggy wrapper, laid it on a plate and told it to wait. He was about to toss the sodden newsprint in the trash when his eye again caught the boldface headline about the very same Duchess of Albanera. The papers did not mean a real, live duchess in the usual sense of the word, but a painting by the noted Italian Renaissance Mannerist Agnolo Allori, a.k.a. Bronzino, depicting Duchess Eleonor of Albanera. The portrait, painted on poplar wood and about two and a half square feet, had disappeared from the State Gallery three days before. "The theft of the artwork," it said in the newspaper, made almost indecipherable on account of the pickle brine, a report on the soccer match between "Slavia" and "Sparta" shimmering through it from the other side and mixing with its coverage of Bronzino—"the theft of the artwork seems all the more futile, given that every art dealer or enthusiast would immediately recognize the painting, thus rendering it unsaleable. Hence the thief can only be an uninformed novice or a madman. Whatever the case, he will be caught." A statement by the museum directors printed underneath this self-assured news item offered the "borrower of this painting" immunity from criminal prosecution if he deposited it unharmed at a location yet to be agreed on. A reward was in store for anyone who could provide the police with any clues as to the whereabouts of the portrait.

Schaschek unpacked his ham, fetched two leftover breakfast rolls from the kitchen sideboard along with a brown earthenware vessel with butter, and began his meal. Chewing, he looked around the room, greeting each and every single object, first the armoire, then the green plush-upholstered sofa, then the bookcase, then the armchair, then the bed and the music stand with sheet music. With each—even the walls—he carried on a kind of dialogue, forgetting neither the geranium on the windowsill nor the wall clock nor the table lamp, and all of these objects answered, first individually, then in unison, so that soon the entire room was filled with Doric rhythms:

> We, the waiting ones,
> always are loyal,
> incorruptible objects.
> We of wood or of iron,
> stone or of bone
> shadow-casting or,
> made of liquefied green glass
> some diaphanous,
> ever servicing objects.

As the music faded away and he chewed and ate the last bites of his meal, cleared the table of plates and cutlery, and pedantically straightened up the kitchen, he slowly produced from his back pocket the ornate key with heart-shaped handle and opened the heirloom armoire, from which he took a wicker bottle with the label "Orvieto." He filled a Bohemian overlay cut-glass cup with the gold-glowing drink. Then he took from the armoire the violin case, and from this the violin, honey-blond, slightly blackened around the grooves, but with the fine sweep of a true Brescian, whose every feminine detail, every line, every swelling served to produce pure harmony. Just tuning it was an unspeakable pleasure, rehearsing and sampling its tones, restoring order and the proper relations undone by the previous night's playing.

Finally, leaning into the deepest darkness of the armoire, he took from it a veiled object, lifted the faded, fleur-de-lis silk scarf, and placed on the fauteuil's velvety softness the portrait of the Duchess of Albanera.

"Your Highness doesn't look too happy today. I admit that for a lady of your station staying in an armoire is a little unorthodox. But for Your Majesty, as well as for me, a whole new era has dawned. Bear in mind that you now have a private life again. Is it really so desirable to be in a gallery under the surveillance of plebian guards, always stuck in the same spot, at the mercy of the curious and shameless gazes of every petit bourgeois who comes along, every adolescent brat, every snobbish schmuck? Isn't that a thousand times worse than being in prison, rightfully or wrongfully, or in a convent, where at least you can live a spiritual life even though it may be against your will? I admit, it wasn't you who chose me, but I who chose you. But isn't this act of daring alone worthy of your appreciation, of being rewarded by you? Have I not wrested you from a wrongful forlornness, from a bitterly foreign place you were carried off to, unasked? Do I not offer you a home, one you may never have counted on, and a modest one for sure, but nonetheless one that is human inasmuch as you are loved here?

"Yes, you're breathing again, I can see it, and you're more real than the duchess you portray, who has long since passed away and rotted in her coffin. You, *una bella*, are still alive in all your beauty. Your inscrutable eyes shine golden light on all creation. Hopes and dreams still stir behind your brow, don't deny it. Your ear listens closely in the hope of hearing ardent confessions. And your hand? Does your hand not reach for your heart, because you still have one to give away? Really, what are all bygone eras in view of your still-vivacious youth? Your dress is sewn with Indian pearls, your fingers sport gold and sapphire. You're a duchess. But the tender roots of your brunette hair, held in place by a pearl net, hint that, should you want to undo it, it would gently and devotedly spill down over your shoulders. And the heavy velvet that seems to serve as your armor, contains—don't deny it—fierce and trembling desires.

"With me you'll live, dear Duchess, because I live with you. In the big museum, which admittedly has something palatial about it, you were merely preserved, kept chemically healthy, a thermometer, barometer, and hygrometer showing the experts that you were doing well. Were you doing well? But here, albeit in a modest environment, you can lead a normal life, may fulfill your duties, might share my joys and cares and are not only given admiration as nourishment but—as it is between human beings—the occasional piquancy of a loving objection or (now, for example) blissful praise, because I can see that your dissatisfaction has vanished and that you're smiling again, maybe not with abandon, but with a furtiveness that shows you've understood me. You're smiling, Eleonor. The dearly departed, who only lived to sit as model for you, cannot do that anymore. We all live, I would venture to say, as provisional models of deeper realities, though not everyone has the good fortune to be cognizant of this."

Schaschek toasted the portrait, thinking this old-fashioned gesture would be timeless enough to seem familiar to the Duchess. Then he began to improvise on his violin. There was still some sheet music open on the music stand, but ever since his life had changed he didn't follow the music anymore. He let the violin play on its own terms. Eleonor listened attentively to this miracle, indeed it almost seemed that her otherwise open eyes were now half closed. But it wasn't she alone who was listening, for his playing carried into the courtyard arcades, muffled by the closed window.

The authorities and the public were clueless as to how the portrait of the Duchess of Albanera had been stolen. It was even a mystery to Schaschek himself. What is certain is that the act of appropriation was not preceded by any elaborate planning. Neither physically nor psychologically had he prepared himself to do it. It was a sudden resolve, love at first sight, the moment he caught a glimpse of the portrait—the savage theft of a woman, *Frauenraub*, the way distant mountain peoples were probably still accustomed to doing it. Schaschek saw the painting, tore it from the wall, covered it with his raglan coat and left the gallery unobserved and through the director's office to boot, which had a side exit onto the street. Anyone else attempting such a feat would have been caught for sure. But in Schaschek's case, just as in roulette, the lone improbable bank-breaking factor happened to be on his side: sheer luck. No one saw him swipe the Duchess; no one was in the director's office adjacent to the gallery; the side exit, otherwise securely bolted, happened to be unlocked this time; and no one was on the street outside, which was a relatively unfrequented side street anyway. With the painting tucked away beneath his coat, Schaschek even went for a leisurely stroll in the nearby park along the riverbank, feasting his eyes on the ever-enchanting panorama of castle and cathedral before heading back to his apartment, in no particular hurry. No one could claim that he hadn't given the custodians of the law ample opportunities to catch him red-handed. But perhaps that was the very secret of his success. He didn't feel the least bit guilty, at most a little bit surprised at himself, and on the whole extremely satisfied. He hadn't planned a thing, because he hadn't even known that the portrait existed before he set eyes on it, and he hadn't entered the gallery with the vague intention of stealing some painting or other, either. Pedantic experts of the soul might have come up with the clever explanation that his intention to conquer this incomparable pinnacle of radiant womanhood had smoldered, dimly or not so dimly, in the darkroom of his conscience ever since childhood, only to flare up irresistibly upon beholding the features of the Duchess of Albanera.

Whatever the case may have been, never in his life, neither at his parental home, nor in his school days, nor on the job, had Schaschek broken a law of any kind. He enjoyed the most unconditional trust of his superiors and his environs. Union Bank would have given him their entire cash reserves for forwarding to consignees in Brazil or Alaska and not a single heller of it would have gone missing. This might be partly explained by the fact that money didn't remotely interest him. He dealt all day with numbers signifying money, and so in his eyes it was degraded. The numbers themselves, on the other hand, numerals in general and the magic of calculability, had something astonishing for him, indeed were almost sacred, so that applying them to possessions and property seemed to estrange them from their deeper meaning. Money, to him, meant ham or salami, and you didn't need much of those.

It wasn't as if Schaschek, as in the case of most trivial art thefts, had been coming to the gallery on a weekly basis to study the portrait, its placement and surroundings, to familiarize himself with the gallery's security system and the habits of the guards, all for the sake of pulling off the ideal heist which he'd planned down to the fraction of a minute. For criminals or fools of that sort, the real fun is the planning and preparing, which is why they're virtually asking to be arrested, are working towards being apprehended sooner or later. Incidentally, the living presence is constantly at feud with such calculated projects. Any attempt to control this life principle would be tantamount to invalidating it. The sudden impulse acting in harmony with nature, on the other hand, always offers the surest chance of success, provided that luck is on your side, without which even the most meticulous planning will lead to nothing, lacking as it does, in any event, the self-evidence of free improvisation. Of course, the aforementioned pedantic experts of the soul might advance the theory that years of complicated projects are subconsciously compressed into the narrow space of seconds. Whatever the case, Schaschek had the Duchess with him for better or for worse—like a lover or, rather, almost like a wife.

The museum director had lived in a constant state of severe melancholy ever since the incident. He was responsible to the "Society of Patriotic Friends of the Arts," which provided his institution with support and funding for ensuring the safety of its works of art. No less displeased was his assistant, especially considering his burdened conscience, having failed to mount the painting in a theft-proof manner. The other exhibits were no more secure. But the effort it would have required to reliably safeguard the existing collection would have cut into the resources for adding and expanding it—a frequent dilemma in other areas of life as well. The missing Duchess escalated the conflict between conservative and liberal members of the "Society of Patriotic Friends of the Arts" (whose spiritual patrons once included Goethe). Indeed, this conflict had reached its climacteric peak. As always, the collective fury of everyone involved began by seeking an outlet where it was bound to encounter the least resistance, meaning that for the time being—and for the sake of reacting at all—the museum guard in charge of the gallery where the portrait of the Duchess had been hanging was fired. It was no use for him to point out that he'd had four rooms to watch over, and that he wasn't omnipresent like the Good Lord was. He had happened to be explaining to a group of visitors the magnificence of his favorite painting, the *Ascension of Christ* by the Master of Třeboň, when the mishap occurred. But the words "favorite painting" were the bane of this unfortunate man. "It's not your job to interpret your favorite painting," shouted the director, "It's not your job to have favorite paintings at all! Your job is to keep an eye out and make sure that nothing gets damaged or even stolen."

"Gets stolen or even damaged," shouted for his part the curator for Renaissance art.

"Words are not the issue here," State Curator Dr Hönigschmied chipped in, "the issue is how the thief could have gotten away with his loot."

"No," the society's treasurer, Count Sternberg, objected, "the issue is how we can get the painting back."

The director's assistant, Herr Ströbl, swore that at no time during visiting hours had he left the office where he was standing in for his boss that day. And he even believed this himself, for he'd completely forgotten that he'd gone to the facilities without, in his haste, making sure that the backdoor to the office was locked. Things like this usually get repressed in such cases. The door in question, which led to a small staircase and from there to the side exit, was—in this the director and his assistant were agreed—naturally always kept locked. These two men were in the habit of entering and exiting the gallery through the main entrance. No one used the side door, which was actually just a kind of emergency exit. It's possible that the assistant (even though he wouldn't admit it) or the director (but he, too, wouldn't admit it) had accidentally unlocked the door, turning the key the wrong way without thinking when carrying out a routine check to see if the door was securely closed. Each of them had a key. And both of them secretly shuddered at the thought that this door might have actually been open for weeks or months on end without anyone even noticing. The consequence of this awkward state of affairs at any rate was that a palpable sense of alienation and suspicion had developed between the director and his assistant, accompanied at the same time, however, by a secret solidarity, because neither of the two was entirely sure—of himself or the other—regarding the question of who was guilty of leaving the door unlocked. Whatever the case, the policemen who inspected the scene of the crime and ascertained the facts of the case found the door locked. And Schaschek, of course, knew he'd passed through it.

"How did the thief pull it off?" pondered the assistant.

"Robbers aren't thieves," shouted the director, "the appropriation of property in the presence of others is robbery and not theft, according to the law."

"But no one was present."

"Baloney! The room is connected with the one where Novotný was blathering about his Master of Třeboň."

"Novotný comes from Třeboň," said the assistant. He suggested hanging a Bassano in the empty space. "It happens to be from around the same period and about the same size."

"For all I care you can hang yourself, Herr Ströbl," suggested the director.

*

"You don't know the least thing about me," said the Duchess to Schaschek. "You know nothing about my childhood and youth, and you don't know how I went on living apart from my becoming an image: as a girl, as a lover, as a wife, and then—what do you know—as a lover once again, as a mother at the same time, growing old and, finally, as a corpse. Don't tell me you've read about me in history books. History books know nothing about real life, least of all about the life of a woman."

"I didn't read about you in history books. I'm not tactless."

"You don't know a thing yet think you love me, you take me as a kind of wife without even stopping to think about it."

"It's always that way between people," replied Schaschek. "You know nothing about my past either."

"Certainly not. But I didn't tie you to me."

"That's debatable. It's always that way with people, and it's no different anywhere else in the world. Two strangers come together and call each other by their names as if they knew each other. The details? They're good for conversation, even necessary for it. But they don't enable you to really know another person. The love of details is bound to decay. Only the love of something whole can last and grow."

"You seem awfully pious, my dear, or at least you act like it. But I see you looking at me. You talk to me too. You play the violin for me. And I know you think of me when you're not around, and surely you dream about me too, because you don't possess me so entirely and wantonly that you wouldn't be dreaming of me. None of that is possible without details. If it were, you could just as well love that blowzy, arrogant wench by Gerard Dou who kept giving me sidelong glances from her window. Even the gallery director, a man otherwise entirely devoid of manners, could see that the situation was inadmissible and moved the petty-minded, vulgar woman to another gallery. Thus, dear Wenzeslaus, only through my being imaginable, only by virtue of my personal attributes can you love me."

"You're very witty, Eleonora, I have to hand it to you. If you'd been born a hundred years later, I bet you would have read Spinoza. And a few centuries later you would have learned that the whole is not merely the sum of its parts, that every detail is co-created by all the other ones as well as by the whole, and that therefore one thing gives rise to the other ad infinitum. But that too is probably not the be-all and end-all. Because life is obviously much more than all of this taken together."

"The way you see me now," answered the Duchess, "and profess your love for me, I don't have hips, thighs and legs. That's part of a woman, you know. My invisible parts could be completely misshapen. Not to mention my character. What do you know about my character? You don't honestly think you can read it in my face, do you? Aren't we women at the height of our beauty endowed by nature with an ephemeral and deceptive mask whose only purpose is to cause men's downfall, and behind which more masks are usually lurking?"

"This, dearest Duchess, was said by Schopenhauer. But I only believe him up to a point."

"*Dio mio!* I can tell you don't have the least experience with women. How many have been loved by you? How many have you bestowed your favors upon? How many have you destroyed? Have many have ruined you? That's all part of the game. My dear fellow, you don't know the first thing about women, and when I say 'women,' I mean women and not some half-baked tadpoles."

Schaschek was silent.

"You see, I told you!" laughed the Duchess. She laughed uncontrollably and couldn't stop, so that it must have been audible from outside on the access gallery. Then her laughter suddenly ceased, and she said, "It's obvious that only a wholly inexperienced person could have gotten into what you did. I even have a soft spot for you because of it. But don't expect too much. Take a good hard look at me. Do you really think that I'm sweet, innocent and devoted? Hardly. I'm selfish and depraved. Believe me, the way women subjugate themselves and a man to their body, so unconditionally, has something gruesome about it. Any man who's slept with one should drive her away the very same night if he doesn't want her to chase him away."

"Maybe," remarked Schaschek unperturbed, "but what you describe can never happen to us. There's nothing to fear, neither me nor yourself."

"Some comfort," muttered the Duchess. "You fool," she then screamed, "I murdered with a dagger and poison. Underneath the sapphire on the index finger of my right hand there's a poison that's more destructive than all the poisons of the Borgias. While painting the ring, the artist Agnolo kissed it, and I was frightened that this mere kiss would bring his death in a matter of seconds. I had a spouse. Most marriages fail, because men marry for different reasons than women, and because every man and every woman discovers before long that life is an utterly lonely place, a loneliness that marriage can barely disguise. The worst thing about it, though, is not the fact itself, but its boundless and ever-recurring banality. My husband thought he couldn't do without me, so I used my ring to help him overcome his loneliness while holding on to my own. What do you say to that?"

"That's pretty much what I expected."

"The whole world knew about it, but I was never accused of anything. I had friends in high places. When I got married the second time, the Holy Father said to me, 'My daughter, don't forget that the key to a good marriage is that everything in it, whatever it happens to be, every suffering, every insult, every guilt and every misfortune can always be made good again.' And I was determined to forgive my new spouse, the Duke, no matter what he did to hurt me. But there was one thing I hadn't counted on. Three days after our wedding night, he left me alone on my silken bed. He betrayed me—with another man."

"So you probably used your ring again?" interjected Schaschek.

"Not at all. I did something far better. I enslaved my husband's lover to my body and worked him to a point that one day, with the aid of God and the Madonna, he thrust a Toledo dagger in my spouse's heart."

"With the aid of God and the Madonna?"

"Yes. In the middle of the act, when he'd gone to bed with him. He was a gifted goldsmith and by nature a God-fearing man. I watched my husband breathe his last. Would you believe I felt almost nothing? Could you see that in my features, my eyes, my mouth? Maybe you could tell from my body if you knew it."

"Well, that's the Renaissance, isn't it," observed Schaschek.

"The painter refused to depict my entire figure. When he finished the portrait after a hundred and sixty sittings, I asked him: 'Agnolo, would you like to paint me as Venus? You may.' He thought about it a while and said: 'I would never be able to paint again.' Then he left and never came back. He was right, of course, and this for two reasons. You see, my darling, that's the way I am."

"Perhaps. But not your portrait. What does that duchess have to do with me? She was a slave to her carnal desires.

But this one here is no slave. Vice, crime and death have no power over her. The painter recognized this, and this is what he wanted to show. Do you think he knew nothing of the abominations you committed or, rather, got entangled in, which basically amounts to the same in terms of higher morality? But it didn't bother him, and it's none of my business either. If I'd wanted flesh and bone I could have had it a thousand times—on the street, in the alleyways, or even at the customary altar. Anyone can do that."

"Anyone? Only if he dares to approach flesh and bone. And that's no easy matter. Because such an individual has to begin by abandoning himself to his own flesh, he has to become completely selfish. And it's none too easy—believe me—to be entirely selfish. You were selfish to the extreme for one brief moment without considering the consequences. That impressed me. But the consequences will be dire. Anyone who does what you did can neither escape unscathed nor with his heart in one piece. You must be aware of that."

"I am aware of that," said Schaschek, "but I'm here for now. And the whole purpose of life, strictly speaking, is to be in the here and now, and postpone as long as possible the inevitable consequences we face, for whatever reason. It's these delays that matter in the end. As long as there's a delay, anything can happen, the meaning of everything you've done, thought, or known before can change completely. You have every right to live with the stolen. Misdeeds flourish for the benefit of generations. Everything is transforming.

Only the dream once dreamt, the happiness lived is eternal and can't be taken back. My reality is alive in you. Who can take you away from me? A museum director? The public? The police?"

"Has it ever occurred to you that someone else might love me more intensely than you?"

"Then it would have been up to him to steal you first. As with any woman, it's all a matter of who gets there first."

The Duchess blushed. "You'll ruin my complexion," she said, angered. "Don't you know that there are very different kinds of love?"

"Mine is mine."

"Marvelous! And how can you be so sure that I don't prefer a different one?"

"Pursue it if you can."

"You know very well that I'm not altogether impervious to your violence."

Schaschek reached for his violin. He plays as if he wanted to capture my entire life, she thought. When he struck up a melody she had the feeling of being reborn, and when he finished, that of blissful death. His solo had the simultaneity of an entire orchestra. His violin seemed to contain all instruments. This amateur doesn't know how artful he is, thought Eleonor; he plays like a maestro, with a naturalness as compelling as the clarity of a children's étude. As if a boy were holding me, his first woman, in his arms for the very first time. The slowly intensifying smile on her face dreamily mimicked that of a Florentine friend of her youth. What were you smiling about, Lisa, when he painted you?—I never smile. What you see is his smile.

Schaschek had left Mader's delicatessen with a degree of apprehension, because for the past few days now he thought he'd noticed a certain reservedness in Ferda, the assistant. It was not only the sequence of salami and ham days that had changed, however, but his purchases on Saturday had also become more voluminous, since Schaschek now stayed home instead of eating out in a restaurant. In short, the structure of his life had changed. At the bank, of course, no one noticed a thing. He kept regular office hours, and the precision of his work was exemplary. But Ferda knew from the Maders' charwoman what her sister-in-law, the janitress Kralíková, had told her: that Herr Schaschek now played the violin every evening and on Sundays, too, and that his playing was extraordinarily beautiful, that, indeed, he played with peculiar fervor, so that not only she herself but a number of neighbors would listen with rapt attention from the gallery. You could hear him speaking too, but he must have been talking to himself, because, despite her extreme vigilance, Paní Kralíková had never seen anyone coming or going apart from Schaschek himself. She even used her master key—so she gossiped with her girlfriend—to enter his apartment twice, but hadn't noticed anything unusual at all, except perhaps for a jar of Krems mustard. But that can be explained, of course, by the fact that the dill pickle season on Rytířská Street is over. As for her, she never buys Krems mustard; it's too sweet for her, and too grainy, and anyway it costs a kreutzer more than the smooth kind. But there's no accounting for tastes, is there. Incidentally, that Schaschek is an incorrigible bachelor. Every Saturday afternoon he has her haul up the week's coal from the cellar and straighten up a bit. He's always around, so she tries to nudge him in the right direction. "Isn't it about time for you to put an end to your being alone? My niece in Napajedl is a marvelous cook." But he always answers, "Paní Kralíková, you can count me out."

The assistant Ferda knew all of these details, and the mustard jar purchased in Mader's store was proof enough of her reliability. Herr Mader himself had felt a repeated urge to ask, "Herr Schaschek, is something troubling you? Is everything all right?" but even his father had trained him that, while any delicatessen-store owner worth his salt should be polite and obliging to his customers when serving them, he should not get involved in their private affairs—apart from their gastronomic ones, that is. Though, mind you, even a comment like "This Madeira has a soothing quality" can be inopportune—because how can you know if a customer wants to soothe himself or his guests? So Herr Mader kept to himself and adhered to the rules of business tact, which didn't go unnoticed by Schaschek, for Herr Mader would always comment on meteorological phenomena whenever a change in the weather occurred; indeed, he considered himself an expert in these matters, what with a professor from the nearby observatory occasionally buying some cod from him and expounding on cloud formations in the process in the hope of getting better service.

One day Schaschek was coming from Mader's store, passing through Havelská Street on his way to Melantrichova Street, when outside Kobylka's pipe and cane shop he bumped into a pedestrian in a most unfortunate way. Schaschek knew the collision was not his fault, for he walked with the very same prudence and precision that he used when entering numbers in his ledger and keeping his files in order. He neither looked up at the stars like Thales of Miletus nor down at the ground like a sniffing dog, and not straight ahead like a horse in blinders either; rather, his gaze was spherical, he took in simultaneously what was going on around him, never touching anyone. Even in the densest throng of people there was always a vacuum around him. This particular pedestrian, however, had stepped on his feet in such a cockamamie and unpleasant way that Schaschek couldn't help but snap at him: "I see you're quite a skillful klutz."

"How so?" asked the pedestrian, offended by the word "klutz" and honored by the reference to his skillfulness.

"Yes, sir," said Schaschek, "with one and the same foot you've managed to step on both of my little toes simultaneously."

"That really is unusual," conceded the pedestrian.

"Indeed. If it had been the two big toes that would be different. They're next to each other. But the two little ones? Can you explain to me how you managed such a feat?"

"I beg your pardon. It was unintentional."

"Wonderful. And I thought you'd stepped on my toes deliberately! Which passerby is concerned about his fellow man these days?"

"I'm not a passerby. I live right here on Schwefelgasse. I don't go out very much. Today, as chance would have it, I had to."

"Nothing but me, me, me," thundered Schaschek, "and why 'chance'? If something is necessary, it doesn't happen by chance."

"Oh dear, you're getting into fundamentals. And in broad daylight on top of it all."

"Why 'in broad daylight'? Fundamentals are fundamentals no matter where or when."

"Does it still hurt?" asked the pedestrian.

"That's not the point. The point is how can you justify your simultaneous attack on both of my little toes?"

"Fine," said the pedestrian, slightly irritated, "I'm guilty. But did you ever ask yourself if maybe you didn't provoke the whole situation yourself? Let's say, by putting your feet in such an unusual position that all I could do was approach you in this singular way. Is the other person always responsible for what he does to us? Are we not accountable to him as well?"

"All I can say to that is that you obviously want to turn the world upside down."

"Not a bad idea. I hope you're on my side. I happen to be a painter. Or, rather, *was* a painter. I gave it up again not long ago."

"Why's that?"

"Need you ask? The world is beautiful enough. You shouldn't go thinking you can make it more beautiful than it is already. But human misery, dear sir! This is something completely different. King Thoas delivering an iambic monologue while the stocking-weavers of Apolda starve? You yourself accused me a moment ago of 'Nothing but me, me, me.' War, dear sir. The Social Question! Universal suffrage!"

"There's more than that," said Schaschek, "and besides: In the midst of the squalor and stench of this world artists have created the greatest masterpieces. Because they wanted to say: This is reality, and each man seeks out his own."

"You're mistaken," protested the passerby, "or, rather, your arguments only apply to a few great individuals. Am I one of them? Are you? Excuse me, I don't mean to offend you, maybe you are one of them. I have too much self-respect to count myself among them. But a person thinks he's entitled to something just because he was born. It's the old dispute with God, do you follow? But, sir, I've sinned. My name is Fürth. My hair's a scruffy mop, because I'm so distraught at my lowliness that I don't even manage to go to a barber. It's true, I stepped on your toes. That could be a profession. In a very complicated way, at that. You could almost make a living from it. From its opposite, too. Take me, for example. I used to restore paintings. But this is pure vanity—shallow and vapid and unproductive. Humanity is going to the dogs. The more numerous its members, the less of it remains. And all you can think about is your feet! When I say feet, of course I mean that symbolically. *Pars pro toto*, a mere part taken for the whole. You reproach me for having bad luck with you. Are you the judge of the world? Most people think they're God-knows-who. Some fool stole the Duchess of Albanera because he didn't have the guts to approach the baker's daughter around the corner. Now he thinks he's got something. But all he's got is his own foolishness—which he had before—and he can't even begin to imagine what havoc he might have caused through his folly."

"Why are you telling me this," yelled Schaschek. "It's worse than getting stepped on by you. And, anyway, it's wrong. The man does have something lasting."

"And what would that be?"

"He dared to do what no one had done before."

"Because no one was such a fool! I know that painting. The eyes. I restored them. They'd almost lost their glow entirely. No one even knew if they were blue or brown. I made them brown."

Schaschek took a swing at him. But the pedestrian dodged the blow, escaping into the dark entranceway of

"Zu den zwei Bären." Schaschek staggered home. He didn't eat. He immediately pulled out the painting and studied it long and hard.

"Why the bright light?" asked the Duchess, "what's gotten into you? You look disturbed."

"A man stepped on my toes. But that was the least of it."

"Did you have a duel?" she asked with interest, "Did you kill him?"

"Nonsense. No one duels anymore these days."

"No sense of honor, how boring," retorted the disappointed Duchess.

"It wasn't the collision itself. It was the things he said."

"He was probably drunk. Did he insult you? What did he say?"

"He talked about war and the decline of humanity."

"How tasteless. That's nothing new. War can hinder peace, but peace can't hinder war. What else can you do to fill the empty hours and the endless infinity of time? And the decline of humanity? Platitudes. I've known princes who lived like slaves. They were slaves at heart. My maids may not have eaten nightingale tongues, but they weren't poisoned or daggered either. In those days that was a prerogative of good society. And yet they looked at me, the one in constant mortal danger, with envy in their eyes."

"Eyes," said Schaschek pensively. "Tell me Eleonor, back then, I mean back in the days before you lived in a painting, what color were your eyes, if you don't mind my asking?"

"What kind of question is that! If you really want to know, I think my eyes changed color. It seems that a person's eyes depend on the eyes of the beholder, especially in the case of women."

"Did something in particular ever happen to yours?"

"Did something ever happen? Something in particular? Constantly. No end of things. Does one not receive the most through the eyes, and give the most through them? The other senses merely take things in. The eye takes, gives, and even creates. It's with the eye that the most happens."

"Surely. But are you certain that your eyes are really yours?"

"And are you certain that your eyes are yours?"

Schaschek fell silent, and the Duchess, too, said nothing more. Her dome eyelids, otherwise visible for just a split second, slowly lowered over her eyes. He observed the sleeping woman at length: The experiences of life had vanished from her features, which now, as so often the case with women, had something childish or at any rate girlish about them.

"Isn't a picture just a likeness of an image?" he asked.

"When Allori painted me," said the Duchess, sighing herself from her slumber, "he confessed to me one day that he'd mixed his paint with tears, and that each of the pearls in my hair and on my dress stood for a night of his grief. There are one hundred and sixty-one of them, and he wasn't lying either, because I sat twenty-three weeks for him to paint my portrait. So please note what the portrait of a woman can mean. Who are you to feel entitled to these tears?"

"Tell me about your eyes."

"Let them be! You want to know too much and don't even know yourself. You think you're courageous. But your daring was a fluke. You say you don't mind if I ruin you. But if you ruin me—this you haven't even considered. You'll kiss the ring on my finger someday and the poison's mere shimmering through a sapphire stone, even just in oils, will have its corrosive effect. You think it's not the worst thing to perish from the poison of a duchess. But what will become of me? I'll wither away in the darkness of your armoire, the wood of the table will rot, and my colors will turn to dust. No one will look after me, and I'll crumble in the hands of the one who finds me. And you would be to blame for my end. Just because you wanted a woman without the natural hazards she entails."

The following morning, Schaschek didn't show up at the bank. The manager waited an hour. Then he went to the director.

"Schaschek didn't come."

"Maybe he's sick."

"That's what I mean. He lives all alone."

"You should check on him."

"I'll stop by on my lunch break."

The manager asked Paní Kralíková which apartment he lived in.

"Herr Schaschek? He left this morning." The manager heaved a sigh of relief. At least Schaschek wasn't seriously ill.

"Do you know where he went by any chance?"

"No idea," said Paní Kralíková. She would have answered the same even if she had known, for it was always safest not to give out information. The manager went back to the bank. "Schaschek is in good health, at any rate," he reported to the director. "I know," the latter replied. "He's been back at his desk for a while now. He had something urgent to attend to."

That same day the evening paper printed the following news item: "The Bronzino portrait of the Duchess of Albanera, whose disappearance was recently reported, was returned to the State Gallery today undamaged. The circumstances surrounding its restitution were just as mysterious as those of its disappearance. While the gallery doorkeeper was in his lodge taking a call on the newly installed telephone, the painting was deposited by an unknown individual on the porter's desk in the entranceway. It was carefully wrapped in an old silk scarf and packed in brown paper. The painting is being returned to its former location and, with heightened security precautions, can be viewed by the public once again, weekdays (Mondays excepted) from nine to four, Sundays from ten to one."

Ferda, the assistant, was about to slice fifteen dekagrams of Hungarian salami when Schaschek interjected: "Ham!"

"Very well, sir," said Ferda, "but if you'll pardon my saying so, wasn't yesterday ham day?"

"Yesterday? Yesterday was a long time ago. But when I say 'Ham!' it's ham day. Or am I not a free man?"

"Surely, at your service," said Ferda. And when Schaschek left the store with his package, the assistant commented to his boss: "It's strange indeed. Very strange. When I put one and two together, the thing with the ham and the salami, his suddenly not eating at 'Zum Prinzen' anymore, his talking to himself, the violin-playing you can hear from the gallery, and the most suspicious thing of all, his remark about being a free man: Taken together it leaves a peculiar aftertaste."

"Delicatessen stores are home to uncommon tastes," said Herr Mader. "The goods we carry are exceptional, which is why our customers are extravagant. Anyway, there's no one in the world who doesn't have their special secret."

So was everything back to normal now? The painting back to where it was before, Schaschek back to his rotating sequence of ham and salami and Sunday roast at "Zum Prinzen"? Was this incident, by all accounts so outwardly and inwardly outrageous, destined to fizzle out into nothing? Hardly. An important point had yet to be considered in the various resolutions to the problem and of which Schaschek knew nothing at first. The fact that museum guard Novotný, referred to respectfully as "Inspector Novotný" by the regulars at his favorite beer bar, did not show up at "Zur Stadt Moskau" on the evening of his dismissal did not seem particularly noteworthy; but his failing to visit his only child, his daughter Gretuška, at the Kateřinky lunatic asylum that very same day certainly did. Each day Novotný had only half an hour between the end of his shift at the museum and the end of visiting hours at the asylum to visit the twenty-year-old girl who was institutionalized there for self-persecuting melancholia. It's the time restrictions that torment people, the time restrictions that cut off the vital breath of those who are hard-pressed anyway and which the fortunate ones are skillful at evading.

Novotný, on that fateful day, had roamed the streets full of grief and shame until it grew dark outside, then—to calm his beating heart—downed a couple of kümmels at a liquor bar, and on his way home got involved in a conflict through no fault of his own and thanks to which he spent the rest of the night at Vyšehrad police station. Suddenly, and without the least instigation on his part, a heavily made-up streetwalker had linked arms with the slightly reeling man right when a policeman, leaping from a doorway just as suddenly, was about to take her away. The lawman grabbed the unknown female so ruthlessly that Novotný protested with some rather unchoice words, which the policeman instantly classified as an attempt to obstruct an officer of the law in the discharge of his duty, giving him a reason to haul in Novotný too. Only in the morning was he allowed to go home, where, sobbing, he explained to his dumbfounded wife the full extent of his misfortune.

Now, Novotný's daily visits to his daughter at the mental institution were by no means merely sentimental in nature but of therapeutic importance as well. It was thanks to these tender-loving visits that Gretuška's condition had been improving from week to week. The feeling of blissful security and an intimate embrace had gradually bolstered and reassured her and had even given the doctors some hope that a certain, albeit tenuous equilibrium might be in the offing. Every day, the girl anxiously awaited her father in the hallway of the women's ward, ached for him like a woman dying of thirst, then rushed at him with shouts of joy when they let him pass through the grated door and she'd spend this half an hour as if she were with a lover, one capable of fulfilling a young creature's every expectation. But this time he didn't come. The orderly tried to calm her with a dozen reasons and explanations, yet the girl fell into a vicious depression; then, while the orderly went down the long and ancient corridor to fetch a doctor and sedatives, the patient rammed her head against the wall, so vigorously that she collapsed and didn't survive the night.

The news of this, which the orderly tried to convey to the Novotnýs as gently as she could the following morning, triggered off a tragic chain reaction, the kind that sometimes frightens us in the case of natural catastrophes or the fates of nations, but that shakes us to the core of our being when it happens to those around us. The girl's mother, who had a heart condition, could not get over this accumulated disaster and a few days after her daughter's burial followed her into the grave. When, after the painting's mysterious return, the museum director summoned Novotný and in a rare fit of human emotion offered to rehire him as a sweeper at least, Novotný looked at him, face twisted in pain, and explained: No, he can't live here any longer. He appreciates the director's good intentions, but unfortunately he has to leave this place. Where to? He doesn't know. He doesn't really care, either. Because anyone as lonesome as he is must feel at home in his loneliness, and it makes no difference where this loneliness is located. But he can't stay here any longer, here where his loneliness was born. "Yes, we're all alone on this earth," said the director, who couldn't think of anything better to say.

Perhaps Schaschek never would have learned of all these sad developments that were prompted by his selfish act because, truth be told, we never really know the misfortunes great and small for which we are deeply responsible. This might even be an aid to human existence, as our consciences would necessarily collapse under the burden of guilt, which at bottom they should. The scale of Schaschek's conscience, at any rate, would never be balanced again. For whoever has had his toes stepped on in a complicated way by the powers of the Erinyes, such a person will never be free again until the final word has been spoken, the final blow has been dealt—which doesn't put an end to anything, however, but is actually just the beginning of the many, countless varieties of despair. He who has run into Walter Fürth on Melantrichova Street shall run into him there again. And it was during this second encounter that Schaschek learned the awful details about the fate of Novotný and his family.

"How is that," he said to himself, freezing with icy fear. "All this time I was living in guilt on account of my hideous selfishness, and I didn't even know it?" He found out where Novotný lived, but the man had already left, destination unknown. Schaschek now realized the absurd extent of his transgression, and that it wasn't about the theft of the Duchess of Albanera at all, not about her and not about him, but by snatching the portrait off the wall he had ruined an entire family and given rise to a Sophoclean tragedy. Maybe it had to come that way. But woe betide him who causes such an offense. His own problem remained unsolved, his daring hadn't remedied his cowardice. It had only ended in disaster.

He sought out the museum director and gave him a full account of what had transpired, sparing none of the details except his conversations with the Duchess. "I would like to be punished, please. I have a right to be punished according to the Criminal Code. Even if I returned the painting unharmed, I'm still a thief, deserving of punishment and atonement."

The director was not at all interested in any renewed publicity for this utterly embarrassing affair. Something seemed fishy about these dubious confessions, and all he wanted was to get rid of this fellow. "Come, now," he said, "you've got some funny notions in your head. Anyway, you've misinterpreted the law. I studied law, among other things.

Active repentance makes you exempt from punishment in this case."

"But poor Novotný!"

"He was right to lose his job. His task was to look after the gallery, and he didn't. And, anyway, we were going to rehire him. He refused. There was really nothing more we could do."

"But what about his daughter? And his wife?"

"His daughter is better off this way. She was incurably ill. And even for his wife, who was only alive thanks to nitroglycerin, it basically put her out of her misery."

"How can you be so heartless?"

The director, who felt this unpleasant conversation had been going on far too long now, stood up, offended. "Let me tell you something," he said. "If you want, go tell the police. But they probably won't believe a word of your story and will end up having you put in a loony bin. We, for our part, are not going to press charges. The case is closed as far as we're concerned. And if there's no plaintiff, there can't be a trial." And with a diabolic glitter in his eye he added: "Would you like to see the Duchess of Albanera by any chance?"

Schaschek fled from the museum. His attempts to mobilize the authorities against him failed entirely. He gave notice at the bank. For health reasons. "But Herr Schaschek, we'd be happy to give you paid sick leave, for as long as you want." No, he would rather go. "But Herr Schaschek, at some point you'll regain your health." "Not me." "But Herr Schaschek, we need you. What will we do without you? You can't just up and leave." "Why not?" asked Schaschek, "after all, I'm a…" He wanted to say "free man" but bit his tongue.

"He really must be in a bad state," said the manager.

Well, it was bad and it wasn't bad. Bad because there was no one he could talk to about the outlandishness, the insolvability and unbearableness of his fate. While talking about things might not exactly save you, it's at least an opportunity to surrender yourself and continue hovering above the abyss, on the fine line between condemnation and absolution. It wasn't bad, on the other hand, because his helplessness and desperation contained the saving grace of penance. Because sometimes he said to himself, "There are misdeeds that can be rectified. But then there are the kind that can't be, ever; the one who has committed them, or even just happened to find himself guilty, can only deal with them implicitly, in the silence of his heart, by virtue of never-ending penance—that is, if he still even cares to be human." And Novotný? Two people go through life and time, one a guilty innocent, the other an innocent guilty man; two people, two hundred people, two thousand and so forth into the millions and billions—guilty-innocent and innocent-guilty, because they are human.

SIEGELMANN'S JOURNEYS

IN HIS FEW BRUTALLY HONEST moments, Siegelmann was willing to admit he was a loser. He hadn't gone far in his profession—one he hadn't even chosen but that had simply overcome him. He had now spent the greater part of his life as the employee of a travel agency without ever having traveled himself, except, that is, to the small country town of Birkenau, barely two hours by train from the capital, and this only during the off-season.

True, he spent day after day, week after week, year after year planning wonderful trips for the fortunate clients of his travel agency—to Sicily or Ragusa, to Norwegian fjords, to the Bernese Oberland, or even overseas, to the West and to the East. True, he knew all the world's coasts and mountains, all the art treasures and health resorts from hundreds of books and pictures, and could have served as a reliable guide and cicerone, on the spot, in Orvieto or even Bombay. In reality, however, and in person, he had only ever known Birkenau and its humble woodlands, excepting of course the city he was born in.

Siegelmann had found employment at the travel agency

after completing grammar school, and abandoned himself to his work ever since. The son of a railroad official, he'd been used to hearing about trips and travels ever since his childhood, even though his father, too, had never been on an extended journey. Not even the fact that his father could have obtained free or reduced-fare tickets for himself and his family ever induced him to travel farther than from the capital, where he performed his duties, to his hometown of Birkenau, where the son—long after the death of his father— was in the habit of traveling too. Siegelmann junior, in his function as a travel agent, was thus continuing the lifestyle and behaviors of his father, albeit at a different level. Even if at work he was organizing the most adventurous travel expeditions—some of which turned out to be the dramatic escapes of high-placed defrauders or the well-prepared kidnappings of daughters from the best families—even if the guidebooks, timetables and flight schedules, the travel posters and illustrated brochures insistently beckoned and enticed him to discover the big wide world, he nonetheless turned time and again to the nearby meadows and hillsides of Birkenau. In the rare moments, though, when he reflected on his own behavior he suddenly grew timid, was filled with despair and glumly regarded himself as a loser. To be sure, he made a living, had his varied responsibilities, and his Birkenau. It's not that he was plagued by an unsatisfied urge to travel that circumstances beyond his control prevented him from fulfilling. Something else was missing. And that which is missing without being definable is always man's greater purpose.

One day a woman in her middle years, a little younger than himself but no longer aggressively young, let her eyes rest on Siegelmann just as she was about to order a book of tickets—for her boss, she said. It was Siegelmann's habit when putting together such a book of tickets to point out the merits and peculiarities of individual locations, even railroad junctions or transfer stations that thanked their very existence to the transport professionals who had called them into being and that for all intents and purposes could claim no real existence of their own. He was well informed about hotels and restaurants of every kind throughout the world, how far it was to the nearest forest or beach, about the luna parks or nightclubs, and how much to tip. He cited the notable persons who had lived, were born or were buried at a certain place or in its environs, and he never failed to praise the good things they had done, no matter how famous these individuals were. Because even if people act like they know it all, it's nevertheless a good idea not to take this knowledge for granted.

"Your boss, madam, really shouldn't pass by Zaunröden without paying a visit to the birthplace of composer Mengewein."

She had never heard of Zaunröden or Mengewein before, and so they began a conversation—brief enough not to hold up Siegelmann's work and distract him from his duties, but long enough to allow him to seem like a polymath. In doing so the eyes of his listener acquired a sparkle that Siegelmann couldn't erase from his memory.

The summer went by, and one evening—it was still light out—it came to pass that Siegelmann encountered these eyes again on his way home from the travel agency.

"Well, did your boss stay on in Zaunröden?"

She didn't know, but she certainly remembered Siegelmann's suggestion.

Since they were now loosely acquainted, he walked her to her front door and on this occasion learned that her name was Magda.

"You've probably traveled a lot," she said the next time they met one Sunday, as the two of them were strolling through the old arboretum. They walked all the way to the river, where they took a ferry to the other side and drank coffee at a Baroque palace that had been converted into a restaurant for day-trippers.

"Traveled a lot?" asked Siegelmann. He didn't dare say "no," although this most likely would have elevated him in her eyes rather than diminishing his status. After all, it would not be unusual that someone had a lot to say about the world after traveling it from one end to the other; but describing it in detail without ever having been beyond Birkenau is quite an achievement. It was not in Siegelmann's nature, however, to utter the "no" so essential and decisive in such a moment. Instead he began to talk at length about the wonders of

Hawaii: its gleaming-white beaches, the slurred and wistful sounds of ukuleles and guitars, the cheerful hospitality whose praises even Chamisso had sung, the pineapples and poi, whose preparation he described in detail. So alluring was this blessed island world that many a man who had merely come for a brief vacation forgot his home, his family, his work, surrendering to this magical paradise and never going back.

"You must have had a strong will," said Magda. And again Siegelmann lacked the courage to admit that his storytelling was merely second-hand knowledge enlivened by his own imagination. He was silent and soaked up her admiration, not so much for himself but for the grandiose picture of Hawaii he painted.

"A strong will, that's true, I guess you need that," he then said. "Just think of the casino of Monte Carlo. How hard it is to tear yourself away! But I've got the knack of it now. You should only allow yourself a small sum, twenty or thirty francs. That's what you should gamble with. If you win, good for you. If you lose, well, it was the price of admission for having fun and gaining some experience. If you really want to play for stakes, I mean risk a sizable chunk of your assets, it can only turn out badly. The many victims of passion, lying around limp and muddled in the cool side halls of the casino, should be warning enough. Those who have wisely bought a return ticket and carry it in their pocket might stagger back to life contritely. Others reach for the revolver, after stealing one last glance from the flowery terrace at the *bleuté immense de la Méditerranée*. Because nature, Magda, plays into the hands of the casino directors. Above the gambling palace the mountains thrust heavenwards, and below they press against the sea. But in the middle, Death receives its guests between the palms and agaves. The Red and the Black, Magda, blood and death. The casino, Magda, a moral institution like the theater. Fear and compassion. And catharsis for some."

"And you yourself, Richard? Did you win or lose?"

"Neither one nor the other," said Siegelmann reflectively, while the two of them sat down at a table with a checkered tablecloth in the garden of the restaurant-palace.

The vividness of his travel pictures grew from one meeting to the next, and he told each story as if he had been there in person. And this is—so he reassured himself when his conscience began to prick him—the most legitimate and impressive way to tell a story. Every poet tells his stories that way, indeed he has no choice but to tell them as if he'd been a key witness to the events he's recounting. Rehashing the experiences of others is dull. You have to have been there yourself. That makes you credible. "I read that certain column drums in Girgenti still bear the burn marks of Punic fire." Who's going to listen if you tell it like that? But if—praise and glory to the indefinite pronoun!—you say: "You can see rust-brown marks on the columns and it makes you wonder just what they are. '*Incendio Cartaginiense*,' says the guard." That's the way to do it. Or maybe like this: "Up above the temple of Girgenti sits a lonely taverna where seldom a foreigner sets foot. In the midst of a tangled garden, it dreams away in the swaying, playful shadows of silvery olive trees. Down below, the gold-brown columns of sanctuaries hover over a sea of deepest lapis lazuli. The whole thing is set in the ring of the heavens, which glows relentlessly and platinum-white. Peasants with dark Nubian eyes and a dash of Saracen sensuality in their protruding lips dismount from their donkeys and enter the garden to take a sip of the mild wine that permeates the body rapidly and deeply, runs through it with exotic spice and kindles the fire of their speech—guard fire, dance fire, altar fire, memories of the fire that Hannibal set in this temple. Was it Hannibal? The temple ruins down below stand like works of nature in this landscape that has something metallic and magnificently bleak about it. It was probably Himilco. But nowadays it doesn't matter. You sit here as a guest. The proprietor offers what he has, as if it were a gift. You would like to pour a libation, for the god you don't know but want to appease. Like a figure on a vase, the proprietor's wife stands in the doorway. 'Goodnight, miss! Good luck to you!' you say when leaving. 'Good luck to you,' she answers, 'I have three children.'"

That would be an eyewitness report, thought Siegelmann. Nosy questions in between would be blithely ignored so the whole thing doesn't become a monstrous lie. For it's easy to give testimony to the great and universal, the more spectacular vestiges of imperishable history. In a certain sense, you're always part of it. It's just with the small and symptomatic details that you have to watch out. That's where you can slip up. But here, too, Siegelmann was much more shrewd than others. His work at the travel agency, his avid reading of the latest traveler's manuals, the *Baedekers* and *Guides Bleus*, and the travel diaries of poets and journalists kept him abreast of all the details. He wasn't easy to trip up. He wasn't spreading untruths. He could justifiably claim that his ideas and concepts of, say, Lourdes or Perugia were far more sound and realistic than those of the individuals for whom he organized train or plane tickets to go to those places. He was even skilled at depicting the inconveniences and embarrassments that various journeys entailed: the mosquitoes and the stenches, the rousing morning cries of donkeys and roosters, the water that stops coming out of the tap only to shoot forth suddenly, boiling hot, and the bothersome contrivances and endless running around when you lose your passport in a foreign country. But everything, even the annoying things, ultimately reveals something. "Waiting for a haircut in New York gives you the chance to do people-watching. A regular customer moseys in with the clumsy step of an orangutan, a fat cigar in his drooping mouth. He doesn't notice anyone. Wordlessly he lowers himself into the swivel chair, extends a hand to the manicure girl while the other holds a newspaper he appears to be reading, he stretches out his long legs to the stool of the shoeshine boy, leans his head back for the haircut—and thus keeps three employees busy at once. The newspaper, which he's now holding over his head almost horizontally, gets unruly and tries to fold in on itself. But he reminds it of its duty with a blasé turn of the hand. And the paper obeys this ill-humored man who's tormented by the Furies of his success." Added details like that can make a report on the Rockefeller Center seem like authentic experience.

Where did Siegelmann get his stories? An exact imagination. Never in her life had Magda heard so much about the world, never had she met someone who could relate their experiences in such a captivating way and who even seemed to be familiar with the most exotic languages. He had been just about everywhere. He tempered the fantastic with the ordinary. And since she soon noticed that he rarely responded to her questions and didn't seem to want to be interrupted, she gladly let him talk and confined herself to listening. He didn't tell his stories with words alone but with a gaze directed off into the distance. At the same time he was very modest. He kept himself in the background. But, lost and lonely as she was, each and every one of his words fanned the flames of her desire to experience the marvelous theater of nature and the arena of human deeds.

Magda was the daughter of a widow who ran a non-descript notions store tucked away on a side street of the city. It didn't carry the basics and essentials but threads, yarns, silks and wools, needles, buttons, hooks and eyes, and dozens of other little necessities indispensable for sewing and tailoring but which in view of the overall piece of clothing humbly stepped off-stage and vanished. And this widow was, strictly speaking, not an actual widow either, but had been abandoned by her husband before Magda was even born; he died shortly thereafter without ever returning to the no longer youthful mother of his child. In other words she was the widow of a man who according to the law was still her husband but in truth and reality was no longer such, because—as is so often the case—the law doesn't always harmonize with truth or reality.

Growing up in an exact world of small things, in which every pin counted, each thread was measured, and each snap was assigned its own container according to size and color, Magda was raised by her mother in the spirit of order and gentle self-limitation, with "Don't forget to say: *Küss die Hand*—Goodbye and thank you" and "Don't talk without being asked." The fact that her father had denied her mother, and hence denied Magda herself before she was even born, was something she would only discover much later, long after her mother's death, and this by chance, which—as usual—had been lying in wait for many years, ready to ambush the unsuspecting woman in the form of a yellowed letter from her grandmother to her mother. The letter, like most letters from grandmothers, not to mention mothers-in-law, would have best been avoided altogether. But it happened to slip out of a prayer book one day, triumphantly revealing the whole superfluous truth and causing nothing but disappointment and grief.

Up until that point in time Magda had believed her mother's stories, who claimed that the girl's father had assumed a leading position in the oil fields of Ploieşti but—before his wife and child could join him—fell victim to an explosion. Now, thanks to her grandmother's letter, it turned out that Ploieşti had merely been a figment of her mother's imagination, the fruit of necessity, of the wish to delude herself and the young child about a very different and loathsome reality, the upshot of which was that this man, devoid of any sense of responsibility, had gotten involved with an all too qualifiable woman and died in a shooting incident at an establishment that likewise left no room for doubt. The affair had caused quite a commotion at the time but had taken place in another city, actually abroad, and so fortunately Magda's mother did not become the talk of the town. She had invented Ploieşti for the child's and her own sake, and with time she even came to believe it. In this way she succeeded in making the father appear in Magda's eyes as a martyr of dutifulness and familial love.

Jealously guarded by her mother, Magda, whose disposition and outward appearance both developed in a pleasing manner, was deprived of all contact with the opposite sex. Her female classmates, too, were an unwelcome intrusion as far as her mother was concerned, for they might have led Magda astray all too easily, to a world where disasters

occurred, like the one that had befallen her. She had vowed
to protect Magda from suffering a similar fate. And although
this protective wall gave rise to the contrary desires to be
approached and touched and magnetically steered in the
finest and the most hidden things, as well as to a desire for
the great wide open, transformation, diffusion, when her
mother died and the painful family secret came out into
the open she was suddenly gripped by a fear and shyness
that effectively counteracted all of these desires. Maybe, so
she thought sometimes, the deeper meaning of the telltale
letter's sudden appearance was to give her a justified warning
against certain dangers and mistakes now that her mother's
care had finally come to an end. And so Magda went her
way, alone.

She had learned a few things, and worked as a kind of
factotum at a law firm. The boss of this defense machine,
which refashioned the accused into a just man with the
help of generous down payments, was ominously called Dr
Umtausch—that is to say, Dr "Conversion." His two clerks
were a very old and a very young man, both of whom were
underpaid on account of their ages. The old clerk was the
true soul of the office. He knew the porous boundaries of the
law, he was familiar with the injustices of the justice system
as well as the justice of injustice. Tiny paragraphs pulsed
in his veins instead of blood corpuscles. He constructed
his boss's pleas in such a way that the state prosecutors,
no matter how sound their arguments, feared for their

reputation if Dr Umtausch took on the defense. His elderly law clerk, old-man clerk, as his younger colleague called him, never so much as looked at Magda. He was neither friendly nor unfriendly towards her. She took notes, typed, ran errands—and that was enough for him. Magda had never heard a private, personal, or for that matter human word come from the old man's mouth.

"I never get involved in that kind of thing," he once confessed to his younger colleague, "considering that almost every desirable woman could potentially be my daughter or granddaughter, I live in constant danger of latent incest."

The young law clerk was already the fourth in a series of young trainees, each of whom had gone or been sent on his way after gaining some practical experience. Dr Umtausch was sizing up his young clerk, with his lone daughter in mind. The current young clerk seemed to fit the bill and knew it. He had an acquisitive eye for the daughter and the practice, and was therefore willing to put up with the meager pay. Young-man clerk, as his older colleague called him, was careful not to pay the least bit of attention to the secretary in the office of his presumptive father-in-law. Anyway, she was several years older than him. And so she sat or flitted to and fro between Dr Umtausch, old-man clerk and young-man clerk as if she were living in a fortress, completely inaccessible and oblivious to the male world, a damsel in an iron tower without a view, just a high little window that allowed her to see a piece of the unmoving heavens. In its fluctuating moments the sky showed her colorful and beguiling fata morganas, which Magda herself was quick to dismiss as weather-related, will-o'-the-wispy sentimentality.

She hastened, seldom looking right or left, through the world outside her iron tower, in the early hours of morning, running the occasional errand, and on her dusky walks back home. This world had inflicted harm on Magda before she was even born, and she took it for granted that further calamity was lying in wait for an unguarded moment. And so she took precautions. But the fact is that all our resolutions and precautions have a limited influence on our fate; the important things have a mind of their own. If a human being wants to live he has to forget himself. Profound encounters take place unexpectedly. And so it is only natural that one day Magda's gaze would come to rest on Siegelmann and—in spite of her background, her upbringing, her suspiciousness—would linger there. There might be gazes we can control. But there are also ones that command us.

Before he met Magda, Richard Siegelmann had had about as much experience with women as he'd had with foreign places, namely zilch. From childhood on he'd encountered women daily, but they basically only existed in his imagination. In this, overall, he was no big exception, if only he had confronted this imagination with reality. Men all too easily forget that their mothers are actually women. It took an ancient tragedian to remind us of the mysterious catastrophes that possibly, indeed inevitably, follow from it. Just as it took a poet to utter the profoundly simple observation that we yearn for the stars while forgetting that we live on one.

Richard could describe the female body in detail, like the ground plan of the Cathedral of Chartres or the layout of a distant city; he took a stroll on it, as it were, and knew its anatomical and functional properties just as he knew what time of day the daily downpours came in Java or when the British Library opened. He had read thousands of novels and psychological studies—written by men—about women: as virgin, wife, mother or whore.

Although he knew about all these things, knowing and getting to know Magda was something completely new to him, something incomparable and disturbing—because it shook the foundations of his carefully constructed and theoretically reinforced notion of "woman," and this by means of wholly incommensurable influences: a faint scent, the inflection of a word, a smile that animated her mouth. Would similar trifles be sufficient to call into question, or even destroy, his established idea of a city or landscape, the ones Siegelmann carried inside his head, the ones he shared with Magda?

His colleagues at the travel agency had all seen a lot of the world, and yet each time they returned from a trip it turned out they'd missed the essential things. How was it possible to be in Rome and not see Villa Farnesina, to fail to visit Stonehenge in England? All they cared about was being somewhere; their travels added nothing new to their lives, didn't change their lives at all. The way his colleagues were married was entirely in keeping with the way they resigned themselves to the world they traveled. You traveled and you married. Once you got married, you were married. Venice? It's gotten pretty expensive there too. And what about Tintoretto's infinitely stooping old men under the voice of God along the Jordan? No, it was too hot for a museum, and we were mainly on the Lido. Yes, but on the strip of land which closes the lagoon and separates it from the sea, didn't you follow the sea on its beautiful bed at ebb-tide, just as it quitted the shore? Did you not witness the wonderful antics of periwinkles and pungar-crabs? Actually, no, and anyway, in terms of swimming, there's not much difference between the Lido and the beach at Hirschberg Lake.

That was the honeymoon of a young coworker, his first trip to the seaside. Of course you couldn't tell that he now slept with his very own wife each night. If the sea didn't impress him, why should his wife? And yet both of them were equally uncanny. But not for Herr Zimtstein. Nothing in this world was uncanny to Herr Zimtstein, neither the things he knew nor the things he didn't. Siegelmann preferred the cottager in Birkenau who had once asked him: "How do you make your living?"—"I put together trips," Siegelmann answered. "Trips," asked the cottager, "what's that?"

Siegelmann didn't quite know if the feelings he had for Magda could be classified as "love." Was there such a thing as a *summa amoris*? There was no way of deciding unilaterally. But he had noticed two things about himself which he attributed to Magda. First, he didn't take himself for a loser as often as he used to, and certainly not a complete loser. Second, he now cared about what Magda thought of him, whereas he used to be indifferent to how others judged him and whether or not they were making fun of him. Magda intimidated him, you might say. "One of these days she might think she's caught me lying. But I don't lie. I merely choose a convincing form for reality and truth. I don't wish to appear important myself, I want the wonders of the world and of life to seem important. I just make the connections, unity expresses itself through me. But what happens if Magda become suspicious about some little detail or other? Details can be dangerous, they're the levers of every disaster."

This concern, which signaled to Siegelmann a change of character, kept him company in the quiet hours. For sure, he was no longer lonely. But could that be taken as a genuine symptom of love for someone of the opposite sex? When he thought about it, it seemed to him that only among his own kind was there hope of not being lonely. A blasphemer—and all interpreters of the Holy Scriptures are none other than this, when you get right down to it—might claim that the biblical God made a cardinal error when he tried to cure man's loneliness by giving him woman as a companion. Of course one might object that God the Eternal made Eve from Adam's own body. *Similia similibus curantur*—like heals like. And so forth to this very day.

To be sure, his relationship to Magda was not exactly passionate, didn't cloud his senses, did not fill him with such an ardent desire that he was forced, for a moment, to forget himself just so he could touch her. Nothing like that had happened in his younger years either. Why should it happen now? But he had noticed that his travel accounts had acquired a particular stylistic verve thanks to Magda, that he had become creative, formed new and astonishing words and expressions, and it even seemed to him that his sentences followed a whole new syntax, one inherent to them alone. And when a person's language changes and asserts its independence, this is generally an irrefutable indication that a change of character is in the making.

Magda had no need to answer for her feelings towards Siegelmann and what he meant to her. Ever since the day when the content of what he was saying was suddenly less important to her than his saying it at all, she knew he was the man of her life. She merely listened, and lost all desire to talk herself or even to ask any questions. Because questions, after all, in their deepest depth are always born of a sense of mistrust. But she did have a desire for boundless absorption. She wanted to trust. She was clearly aware of the intensification going on in Siegelmann's presence, that his storytelling was becoming more rich and lavish. And she too received and gave, the very best a person can give.

Nevertheless it was she who suddenly and unexpectedly posed the fateful question: "And where are we going on our honeymoon?"

It was sudden and unexpected because up to that point neither of them had even broached the topic of marriage or a wedding. And, anyway, according to custom, it should have been the man to pose a question like that and dissolve the mutual restraint between them. The woman would have to act surprised, astonished, possibly even stunned, shed a few tears and then answer, "Yes," a monosyllable which in this case is best when whispered in a low voice, the semi-consonant at the start disappearing to express a fully vocalized sense of well-being. But Magda knew nothing of these sacred rites. She had also completely forgotten at this moment what her mother had always drummed into her: "Don't talk if no one asks you to."

"Yes, well, the honeymoon," answered Siegelmann in a completely businesslike tone, as if he were speaking about a matter they had long discussed, one there was no good reason to doubt. "Most people, like my colleague Zimtstein, travel to Venice, which for centuries has generally been considered an auspicious start, and where there is in fact a huge amount to see and admire. But, I ask myself, is that really appropriate to the actual occasion? You might say the Zimtsteins would have been right to let art be art for once this time. But they'll do it every time. Those who marry think they need a wonder of the world as a backdrop or a counterweight—Venice, Niagara Falls, the sequoias."

"Incidentally, California," Siegelmann continued after a pause, thus giving his words the nature of a court plea, "California has much to be said for it. The giant redwoods I mentioned already, whose tops seem to soar to such immeasurable heights that their treeness can only be made out in the bark of their trunks, the base of their roots, and the smell of pine resin, these trees with their three- or four-thousand-year-old rings are virtually symbols of eternal life. The ephemeral calliope hummingbird and sapphire-colored blue jay whizz between them. Western civilization comes to a jerking halt, as it were, it's suddenly behind you when you reach the coast—you're finally rid of it. You go through nothing but meadows of gold, through agate cliffs, the surf with its bleating sea monsters before you. And yet, what's the use of it? We can't think that far now. Let's choose a middle way, my darling, a middle course between Venice and California. That would be my Birkenau."

It should be noted here that he had never before called Magda "darling" and that she had never seen "his" Birkenau. And yet how tactful it was of him to insert the word "darling" as a kind of self-evident truth, thus legitimizing, so to speak, her rash and almost brazen question about their honeymoon destination. But even if she'd been to Birkenau, this would have made no difference at a moment like this. She would have recognized Siegelmann's Birkenau under any circumstances as the only and most magnificent possibility. She knew that Siegelmann's proposal was not due to any kind of poverty. If California was too expensive, one Venice more or less wouldn't really matter to such a well-traveled man, given the momentous occasion. He wanted to flatter her with an idyll and not oppress her with the gigantic. It was a tender gesture, really. Siegelmann himself, though, was panic-stricken by the possibility that the Venice of his dreams and its fantastic topographies would be overpowered and annihilated by reality. Pretending in front of Magda that he'd been to Venice a dozen times would not have been the problem. The real problem would have been that this world would no longer be his own; and of him there would have been nothing left but Richard Siegelmann, travel agent, who abandoned Birkenau without saving Venice. Much worse: Who would have sacrificed his genuine, higher and magical Venice to a naturalist version, a sham being propagated as reality. He was the skipper of his boat, which took him to all harbors. He was alarmingly intimate in dealing with his sailing vessel, like with a haughty and beautiful woman that no mere mortal can approach but who, for some strange reason, is submissive to her captain. Alas, his ship was in a bottle. He no longer knew how he'd gotten it inside. And to get it out, he'd have to break the bottle.

They were married in a civil ceremony. The official muttered his sentences as if it were a requiem, and without so much as looking at bride and groom.

Afterwards they went to a restaurant called "Zum Prinzen." Dr Umtausch, the best man, felt he should propose a cheery toast. "Just like in the lottery," he explained, "where only one can hit the jackpot, a few get lesser prizes, but the overwhelming majority ends up drawing a loser, so it is with marriages, too. So prove, ere thou'rt forever bound, if heart the kindred heart have found. Because it is forever, or at least lifelong, despite divorce. And even if you do get a prize, it all depends on whether or not you know how to use your winnings properly."

Siegelmann had hinted at his marriage in the office yet did not disclose where the honeymoon would be. He had no desire to hear any disparaging remarks about Birkenau. The newlyweds reached the station towards evening. There were no more summer vacationers. The deciduous trees were at the height of their color, the spruces had added abundant sepia and Prussian blue to their deep-green background hues. The forest had seemed to move closer to the town, which always happened when the city dwellers fled.

The couple lodged with the Kalmus widow, whose husband had purchased from Siegelmann the small mortgaged house of his recently deceased father, under the condition that an attic room be reserved for him on a lifelong basis. Herr Kalmus passed away soon afterwards, and so Siegelmann continued to feel at home in Birkenau, because even the furniture had belonged to his father.

Of course, the second bed that Frau Kalmus had put in the room disturbed the room's previous harmony, the two beds more or less dominated the room completely now—high country beds with thick, fluffy pillows and big, bulging duvets, whose dependable warmth in this advanced season Frau Kalmus had effusively praised. The two began to unpack their suitcases, each on their own bed. They did so in silence and bashfully. There was only one wardrobe and dresser. For the first time a feminine breeze wafted between Siegelmann's mannish, if not to say boyish things, which cowered in a corner, dismayed, and sought refuge in remote drawers, even though Magda's garments did not take up much space. She had taken her finest for the occasion, openwork lace and silk, form-fitting outfits in pastel tones, the fragrant and poetic, which now kept company with Siegelmann's realistic underwear. These timid glimpses into reciprocal worlds were actually their first physical approach, which up until then had scarcely progressed beyond a goodnight kiss at the front door.

Having finished unpacking, they both looked around to see what else there was to do. They weren't in the mood to talk, but they weren't really silent either, they simply avoided speaking. They each sensed that their old way of being together had now come to an end. Anxiously they groped for words to break the ice, but always recoiled, because it had to be completely different than before, an entirely new language. Only when Magda saw a number of travel guides on a shelf did she ask in spite of herself: "Souvenirs from your travels?"

"Souvenirs? Fetishes? Idolatries? The thinking man always knows in advance what he will have to remember."

"But there are things you can only find or buy at certain places. Seashells, corals, rocks. You can use them as paperweights, to keep letters from flying off your desk."

"I never get letters."

"Well, not just letters. Maybe documents, or bills."

"The wind can blow them away for all I'm concerned."

"Still. Something always remains from a trip."

"Surely. But you shouldn't test me," he remarked irritably.

She fell silent. It was quiet in the room but even quieter outside. The window was open, yet the estamin curtain was motionless. The air had a hard time breathing through it. A tardy storm, the rearguard of summer, noiselessly lit up the sky above the woods.

"Listen," Siegelmann suddenly said, "I've never taken a trip before."

She laughed. "You just want to tell me that this is your first real trip, and that the others, however nice and adventurous they were, don't count."

"You're mistaken," he gasped, "I've never traveled at all."

She sat down in an old rocking chair next to the tiled stove, began to gently rock back and forth, and all she said was "Ploiești." And as if this word was the only one she could grasp, she began to repeat it over and over to the rhythm of the rocker.

"At first I thought I could get away without a confession," continued Siegelmann. "Just this morning, before the ceremony, I thought I was strong enough. Before we entered this room, I hoped to keep weaving you into my dream-world, like ornament on brocade."

She stopped rocking for a moment and stared at him in disbelief. Then she began all over again, an interminable "Ploieşti."

"Cut it out!" he yelled. "It's not like that. It's different. You might be thinking: Why today of all days? Why now? Well, let me tell you, it was your things that broke me down. Not some kind of sudden insight, considerateness or even love. To hell with your 'Ploieşti'! It's the little things that did me in. The way you pulled them out of your suitcase, one by one. They belong to someone else, not me, these utterly foreign things. All these containers, vials and tubes, stubbornly insisting, 'We're reality!' It's as if they've conspired against me, all these unbearable silk blouses and scarves. They've made me too cowardly to even be a coward. 'We're real, how about you?' they say. 'We belong to a real person, and you'll be part of our lives now. Are you as real as we are?' I beg you: Stop singing!"

Indeed, while he was speaking and she was ceaselessly rocking, she had put the word "Ploieşti" to a melody.

"And I want to confess something else," he started again. "Sometimes it dawned on me that you knew or sensed that all of my stories were mere fantasies or, let's say, lies, and that your feigned belief was an even greater feat of acting than my feigned experiences were. Why did you smile when I told you about the tavern-keeper's wife in Girgenti, where I've never been? You were humoring me when I turned the light on in my globe so it looked like a lamp. Admit it! You basically knew that I'd never been farther than Birkenau."

"Ploieşti, Ploieşti," she crooned, rocking like a lullaby.

"My father said that women knew things without even asking or learning or doing them. Even the simplest of them is a sibyl. She carries something within her, he said, that comes from time immemorial and points to eternity, and it's from this point that she lives. How did my father, a mere railroad official, know that? Mind you, he didn't say that until after my mother died. So tell me, which of us was stronger from the start: me, with my Hardangerfjord and Mont St Michel and Sugarloaf Mountain in Rio, or you, who knew that there was nothing behind it but Birkenau?"

Magda got up. "Who *are* you?" she asked. "Richard Siegelmann, travel agent at Schenker, someone whose world has fallen apart. Who are you? A poet without a poem, a bricklayer without a trowel. You are who you are. But you were more when you created the world. I'll be going on a journey now."

He didn't try to stop her, even though the storm was fast approaching and a sudden gust of wind blew drizzle into the room.

"It's often like that with newlyweds," said Frau Kalmus, doing her best to cheer up Siegelmann. "Only that which becomes routine is useful in life." She brought in tea with rum. Outside, thick cords of rain began to lash the landscape, lightning crossed the sky, and dreadful, merciless thunderbolts ricocheted from cliff to cliff. And as is common in the countryside during storms, the electricity suddenly went out. Frau Kalmus came back with a burning candle. She sat down with Siegelmann, who had left his tea untouched. "She'll come back, don't you worry," she prophesied, "she's probably holed up somewhere. Nowadays girls run off so easily, but they come back just as easily. Back in my day, things were different. They used to say: Be good at something and be somebody, and any girl will be happy with you. To be somebody, that meant doing what you wanted. And being good at something, that meant feeling certain that luck was on your side, no matter if your job was swinging a hammer or setting watch springs. That kind of man was good enough for any girl, even if she was the empress. And a man like that didn't need to talk much."

That was it, thought Siegelmann: too much talking. A man who is nothing has to talk. And because he's nothing he has to invent things. And now he'd owned up to it, had reduced himself to the minimum. Wasn't that better than a phony maximum? Wrong. That which makes an overabundance phony cannot make an ounce of self-awareness more genuine. The pendulum's still swinging.

The storm now reached that magic height where total pandemonium suddenly yields to stillness, as if the elemental powers had rallied themselves to a final, tremendous verdict. The roar of the downpour is no longer articulated but a uniform and barely indistinguishable mass. You're full of trepidation, knowing you're in the eye of the storm and the worst is yet to come. Like a choleric showering his victim with a flood of invective then pausing unexpectedly at the peak of his anger and looking around with a grimace of resentment and laughter, not because he's about to stop but to let out his entire accumulated animosity in a single, terrible blow, it was thus that in the excruciating silence the final gigantic bolt of lightning came crashing down, glaringly yellow, jaggedless, with the gruesome precision of a demonic harpoon and the concentrated explosiveness in which the prehistoric still roars at us.

Then the electricity came back, spasmodic and uncertain. Frau Kalmus stepped into the doorway and called out in all directions: "Frau Siegelmann!" Then she went back upstairs to him and shook him out of his torpor. "Maybe if we call her by her maiden name. It's her first day, after all."

"Maiden name," he asked, behind the fists he was propping his head on, "Arethusa, Pocahontas, Galatea." And he muttered a long string of names like a poem. The woman shuddered and left.

With the first flush of morning she returned. The candle had burned out, the electric light bulb glared senselessly into the morning light. "Come on. We have to take a look around—ask and search." He got up compliantly and without a word, walked behind her on the paths he knew from childhood. When they came upon a stream he let her guide him by the hand, and when they came to a house he stood at the gate and waited till she returned, always with the same news that no one had seen a female stranger. They walked clear across the vast forest, wet and sunny, as if they were on a hike, Siegelmann bringing up the rear, Frau Kalmus calling out and encouraging him to do the same. But he droned the most peculiar names, tried to snatch the season's last mourning-cloaks, collected hairy-cap moss or turned over stones and engrossed himself in the hustle and bustle of ant colonies. This is how they walked.

Late in the afternoon they reached the narrow river valley, where the waters had dug their bed between closely overhanging sandstone rock formations. The rocks rose pillar-like, some of them imitating the heads and bodies of giants, which is why in popular parlance they were admired and feared as the "wedding procession." The rocks reflected a variety of colors, the cracks were filled with ferns and underbrush, a tiny spruce perched on the occasional shoulder, and the "groom" held a little white birch stem in his extended hand, as if it were a candle.

But during the night something had happened that made Frau Kalmus's blood run cold. The stony bride, who normally followed the groom, had broken out of the bridal procession and now her rocky limbs lay shattered across the stream. There was a gaping hole between the groom and the wedding procession, through which the forest on the other side could now peer into the valley. The lightning's coal-black trace of terror was clearly visible along a broken-down trunk, having knocked a tree right out of the cliff and blasted through the crag. The imperturbable water, however, collected silvery-cool around the shattered limbs of the bride, caressing her torso, pouring past her, creating cascades and waterfalls, and was already busy forming a new, wild and exquisite nature motif.

"Laughing Water," said Siegelmann. "I'm finally in America."

"America," said a horror-stricken Frau Kalmus.

"Nothing is far away," said Siegelmann.

BORDERLAND

IN OBERPLAN AND THE VILLAGES of the Bohemian high forest there were still people by the name of Stifter, even at a time when the poet had become so famous that it almost seemed incredible if someone said their mother or grandmother had actually met him in person. And when violence—of various stripes but equally senseless—later took possession of this landscape, there were still people living there called Stifter, until they too had to go, disappearing to unknown, distant places.

But before that happened I knew one too. He lived in an old house near the village of Glöckelberg, at the edge of the forest that stretches across the slope of Hochficht Mountain then continues to Plöckenstein Lake, then up to Dreisessel Mountain, then on to the northwest in endlessly undulating waves, dark and insistent, along the border of Bohemia.

This man, Anton Stifter, didn't know if and how he was related at all to the family of the great Adalbert. He had neither read anything by him nor did he even suspect that a man with the same last name had consecrated this landscape in a special way by coming from it and loving it.

Anton Stifter was a cottager. His wife had died on him and he lived with his twelve-year-old daughter, Ottilie, or Otti for short, at the steep part bounded by the woods on the one side and by a narrow flume on the other. The flume, which once served to transport felled logs, was now just a narrow, neglected watercourse, useless to all but the frogs and dragonflies, the swift water spiders and the buttercups growing rampant between the mossy, brittle stones of the wall. A good and sensible use, you might say. The house included a meadow that was less than optimal for human needs; scythe and sickle were constantly striking the countless chunks of granite in the ground, with the occasional erratic boulder lying around as well that no one was able to move and that must have stemmed from the time the mountains were formed by nature or God.

But there was one spot where Stifter Toni, as they called him, was able to put in a tiny potato patch, just big enough for the bare necessities. He had a few heads of cabbage too, along with a goat and some chickens, and a stray dog by the name of Skinny. But his realm was actually much bigger than many a wealthy city dweller's, no matter if the latter had safety-deposit boxes stuffed with elaborate, steel-engraved bonds. It included the forest, which was his for the taking, the forest with its varied multitude of berries, mushrooms, fallen wood, grass, and sometimes—there's no need to hide it now—a hare. It included a babbling trout-brook that passed beneath the flume and continued to the

Vltava Valley. It included a clear view of the gentler, rolling hills that stretched into the vast Bohemian countryside. And it included the sky, with its cloud gatherings and weather happenings, white or gray on uniform days, pitch-black and dandelion-yellow when a storm was brewing, forget-me-not- or bellflower-blue, or apple-green, or cockscomb-red in the evening. And it included the hundred thousand sounds and noises that the wind, the water, the animals, as well as many other things moved by unknown powers ceaselessly produced in all variations and keys.

Then one day someone entered this infinite kingdom, and this someone went by the name of me. To the outside world he may have had other names, but that's irrelevant. I came from the capital of the crownland, and I knew a good deal about this forest from my father's stories as well as from books. In a way I knew more about it than Stifter Toni did. But only in a certain way. Because he lived with the forest the way one lives with his father and mother, brothers and sisters, wife and child; he'd been born there to the cries of the jays, the racket of the finches and the tapping of the woodpeckers; he'd been nourished by it and drank its water; he knew its amusements and oddities like you would those of a spouse. I, on the other hand, knew more words and designations. I knew that feldspar was also called orthoclase, that water was H_2O, and that dandelions belonged to the Compositae family, also known as asters. Yet neither Stifter Toni nor Otti were concerned with such classifications.

They dealt with the things of nature with an inborn trust or mistrust, whatever the case may have been, depending on whether nature was friendly or unfriendly towards them.

I came one summer day and asked if I could live with them.

"Live here, sure," said Toni, "but there's just a room in the attic and a straw mattress, and for food we've only got potatoes and sour goat milk, unless you go to Kari's tavern."

I was happy he didn't stand on ceremony. He addressed me with the informal "*du*" and let me use the polite form "*Sie*." Little Otti used the formal, old-fashioned "*Ihr*" when talking to him. He didn't seem to care one way or another if people called him "*Sie*" or "*Ihr*." He himself, in any case, always used the familiar "*du*," even when talking to rocks, to the stream, or to the most important things. "*Du verflixte Hacke*"—you lousy hoe—"you've gone and made yourself dull again." He even said "*du*" to much higher things, to Hochficht Mountain or even to God.

To get to the village and Josef Kari's tavern you had to walk a brief half an hour along the flume and through the woods, a tall and ample stand of spruce trees which gave a rather cheerful impression, what with the light that shone through the trunks in the daytime and the moon and stars peeking through them at night, and even in total darkness when the sky was overcast it exuded a kind of coziness, because behind this piece of forest you knew there were meadows and the village.

145

At the tavern I made an array of acquaintances. First of all the proprietor himself and his pudgy wife, who wiggled her arms like wings when she walked; then some forest dwellers, the most clever of whom was a certain Hochholdinger, skilled at cards and a hard drinker who could hold up to forty half-pints. He had a whole brood of children and liked to sing a song he invented himself:

> From Glöckelberg I am,
> And like my fun as ev'ryone knows,
> My trunk is full o' children,
> Can't get the lid to close.

Then there was the cobbler Poferl, who had a very innocent face but knew by heart the smugglers' paths into nearby Austria and Bavaria. Another regular at the tavern was the American Feiferling.

Feiferling had earned the name "the American" because of a lengthy stay in the New World, where after the turn of the century he had worked for a while as a cigar roller and railroad man. Then he returned to his native village to live out his life alone as a bachelor, in a house that he'd inherited.

"Didn't you like it over there, Herr Feiferling?" I asked.

"I liked it well enough," he said, "but at some point you've got to come home, don't you."

He didn't have a proper profession. He lived off his savings, and his main occupation was doling out advice: "In

America we turn the keys in our doors to the right and not to the left." Or: "In America we write the number one without a tail in the front and the seven without a line through it." Or: "In America we don't have to register with the police." But sometimes he would tell a real story: for example, how he'd once spent the night in an abandoned farmhouse in the forests of Vermont and played with a dog in the darkness, which later in the morning turned out to be a bear. Some people said he told tall tales, but others said that in the expanses of America anything was possible.

In front of Stifter Toni's house, where I was living, stood three spruces right next to each other, higher than the house and much, much older. The house had been placed in front of these three spruces on purpose, for they covered the weather side, protected against snow, and served as lightning rods. One of them had taken a hit once, leaving a char mark all the way down the trunk. Underneath the trees was a jumble of wildflowers that had once formed a flowerbed but now grew every which way without a care in the world. Toni toiled away in the fields or the forest, and there was always something to fix, a shovel handle to be fastened in place, or a shingle to be nailed down. He also had to cook, a chore he shared with Otti. Hashed potatoes with grated cheese was a feast. Otti had to tend the goats, toss some feed to the chickens; she had to knit, which she did quite well, and she had to wash and scrub, for she had no choice in the matter; had to gather berries and mushrooms, pick up wood, haul in a pile of hay—a task she and her father took turns with. In short, there was a lot to do and maintain in this poor but sprawling household.

I myself helped out a little, albeit more for my own amusement, if you can even call what I did helpful. For example, I whitewashed the entire living room, at my own expense, built a wooden bench and table that I placed underneath the spruce trees, and paved the path from the house to the flume with flat stones I'd collected from the hillside with a wheelbarrow.

"Looks like Prince Schwarzenberg's place," said Toni, and it was impossible to tell if his words expressed approval or disapproval. He paid no attention to what I did, didn't bother me when I was writing, and Otti, too, was respectful of my endless scribbling, would delicately walk in on her tiptoes when she came to the attic to hang up garlands of dried mushrooms, even though you couldn't hear her anyway, because she was always barefoot. The drying mushrooms gave off a deep, aromatic scent all around me, and it smelled a bit like petroleum too from my lamp; then there were the odors of forest, of resin and humus, that came in through the window and the cracks in the wall. The dung heap down below added its own special note.

Otti was an odd child. I first noticed this when she was sitting on a granite boulder in the meadow along the edge of the forest. On the hand of her outstretched arm sat a wood-land bird, a bullfinch, so it seemed to me, shimmering-pink and bluish. It chirped a little then flew away, only to come back after a while and sit down on her hand again. I was more than a little astonished that a girl could tame a wild bird, but I didn't dare get any closer for fear of disrupting this little game. Another time I saw her bend over a piece of quartz and pick it up; the stone seemed to shine in a curious way, dark purple, as if it were an amethyst, but maybe it was just a stray beam of light that had somehow managed to get inside. Yet another time—and this time it was very conspicuous—I saw the child standing before a mullein. Holding her hand above it at a considerable remove, she gently waved the hand in the air until the plant began to follow her movements, swaying back and forth, even though there wasn't the slightest breeze. And then I saw her crouch-ing at the stream with her hand in the water. This time I got very close. The child looked up and put the index finger of her other hand over her mouth, as a sign that I should be quiet. She had opened the hand in the water, and I saw a trout approach and stop inside her hand, which closed as if caressing it, without the silver miracle fleeing; indeed, it seemed eager to snuggle up to her hand, which Otti then opened, gently releasing the fish.

"How do you do that?" I asked.

"I just do," she said, explaining nothing.

"You could catch some fish for dinner."

"No," she said, shocked. "Only father with his fishing pole."

"How do you get the fish and birds to come to you like that?"

"The hares, too," she said, and ran away.

Sometimes she accompanied me on my walks. There was one route that went along the flank of the mountain, halfway up, that offered sweeping views through the forest aisles, clear into the Vltava Valley. Another, the Seitz path, penetrated higher and deeper into the woods, where red deer occasionally darted past, black grouse could be heard, or where motionless silence prevailed in hidden places, a silence which—if you strained your ear—turned out to be made of a million voices. Or we went to the "Cholmer," a dark-green pool of water in the middle of the woods. There she would sit down at the edge of the water, where the lilies were, and lean forward. I wanted to hold her back to keep her from falling in.

"Don't," she said. "I'm talking."

And it was wondrous how the moist, wide-open blossoms came closer and closer to her. Yet she never would have plucked one. Sometimes she would stop in front of a spruce, point to the ground, and say, "There!" There was nothing visible except brown needles and moss. But she bent down and dug away the humus a little until an entire family of young, white-brownish mushrooms appeared, which she carefully placed into her colorful scarf. At other times she would suddenly stop in front of a fern, study the leaves for a while then say, "Rain!" And although the sky had been clear and bright, it would soon get dark and rain would fall. She never ran away from the rain, but received the drops like a thousand caresses. We went up to the Stingelfelsen, a cliff from where you could look out over into the Austrian forests and, to the left, at the castle ruins of the Vítkovci. Sometimes she would look hard at the Danube plain, raise her hand and say, "Now!" and in the distance you saw the Alpine glacier suddenly flash blue-white.

Some days I sat on the bench I'd built and, feeling light-hearted, would hum a tune to myself or whistle quietly. She might listen for a while then say, "Hurting?" I'd stop whistling and didn't know if I was sad now because of what she'd said or if she'd noticed, despite my whistling, that I'd been sad all along.

She never spilled a drop of anything, nothing she ever carried broke, everything she did was almost inaudible, and objects seemed to eagerly obey her. She just needed to sing to them now and then, not songs or melodies I'd heard before, no sentences that made any kind of sense, but something like this:

> Broom . . Bench . . Ground-deep . . .
> Bench-ground . . High-ground . . .

Or in a completely unintelligible language:

> Ameta .. Pumeta ... Pumerover ...
> Ashes .. Alfish .. Anteclover ...

Sometimes it rhymed and almost sounded like an incanta-
tion if she sang while going about her chores, sweeping
out the room, scrubbing the pots or firing up the stove. If
I happened to misplace something, a pencil or a book, and
was rummaging around my attic or the downstairs room
trying find it, Otti gave me a quick glance then proceeded
with unerring accuracy to where the sought-for object was
hiding, took it from among the other things and handed it to
me. And when I'd carelessly closed a book without putting
a bookmark between its pages, she would take it and open
it with a single movement to precisely where I had stopped
reading, pointing to the paragraph.

"Does she go to school?" I asked the teacher Macho.

"No, she's sick."

"What's wrong with her?"

"We had her here when she was six. But she never
adapted to the other children. We tried it over and over,
each year. But her behavior is bizarre and she always gives
the wrong answers."

"What kind of answers?"

"If you ask her, for example, 'Who created the world?'
she'll say, 'I created the world.' Of course all the children
start laughing, and the whole lesson is disrupted. When
she's supposed to pray the 'Our Father' she says, 'Our

Mother,' and it's impossible to make her change it. I tried to teach her reading and writing. I didn't succeed. If I tell her, 'Write the word: sun!' she points with her finger out the window but refuses to write it down. When she's supposed to read, she takes the primer, glances at it, but says something completely different from what the book says, sometimes completely senseless words, and all the children start to laugh again. Or, right in the middle of class, she starts telling a kind of made-up fairy tale. Once, all of a sudden, she jumped up from her desk and yelled, 'Fire!'—'Where?' I asked her.—'In Hüttenhof,' she said. Hüttenhof is at least a half-hour's walk from the schoolhouse. Strangely enough, there really was a fire there. But how can you teach a child like this in the same classroom with the others? All the children shun her, no one wants to sit next to her or play with her."

I asked the pastor, "Does Otti go to church?"

"Sometimes," he said. "Toni brings her a few times a year. He's an oddball himself, if not to say downright unchristian. With a girl like that, though, it isn't easy."

"How does she behave?"

"She doesn't sing with us, she doesn't pray with the others. When she's supposed to kneel or stand during Mass, you always have to nudge her first, and then she doesn't necessarily do it. There's always the danger that she'll butt in right in the middle of the liturgy or homily, and shout: 'The wind is coming.' or 'A deer is running.' She turned

my Scripture lessons upside down. For a while I tried individual instruction, but you can't get anywhere with her. A
doctor from Krummau examined her and asked her a lot
of questions. In the end he declared her abnormal. What
a shame!"

I brought up Stifter Otti at the tavern.

"She's nuts, that girl," said Hochholdinger.

"But not particularly dangerous," said cobbler Poferl.
"Been that way since her mother died," Hochholdinger
added by way of explanation. "Talks gibberish ever since.
A girl like that, without a mother, is no end of trouble."

"She's something special if you ask me," said the
American Feiferling, who added after giving it some thought:
"I read something once about a magnetic girl who attracted
lightning."

Otti's father, Toni, took his daughter's eccentricities for
granted. "Is it gonna rain?" he'd ask her. "Go find some
mushrooms," he'd tell her, or: "Get some cress." It never
occurred to him that she'd come back empty-handed. Or
if she suddenly paused and listened while drying the dishes,
he'd say, "Here comes another one." And what do you know,
Skinny the dog began barking a few minutes later and, down
by the flume, someone walked past.

Otti seemed both older and younger than other twelve-
year-olds. She was certainly a beautiful child, not thanks to
any specific features but to their harmonious whole. Her
entire body took part in every one of her movements; with

every glance, her perfect being resonated. When she spoke it was not just her mouth but everything about her that did so, and often her eyes said enough.

When her father came home, tired from felling trees or doing some odd job, she knelt down next to his chair, took both of his hands in hers and looked at him. A few moments later he'd be refreshed. He was so used to these things that he'd come to expect it. She had done this with me several times as well, with the same effect.

That's the way Otti was, and I, too, grew accustomed to her special manner and peculiar talents. Some things are inexplicable; we have no choice but to accept them. The incident with Ludwig, for instance, the little village boy who'd gone missing and was nowhere to be found one evening. He must have gotten lost in the woods. The forest never seemed too threatening at first. But the forest was endless. There were boulders that a child could fall from and hurt himself. There was Cholmer pond, and just a two-hour walk away the lake—and the lake was deep. There were primeval tree trunks that suddenly fell. And there was much, much more that you normally didn't think about but which suddenly seemed menacing to an agitated mind.

It was late at night. Ludwig's parents had already asked around everywhere. Groups of villagers combed the forest, brandished lanterns, called and shouted. They came to us, too. Neither Toni nor I knew what to tell them. Only Otti, whom no one had asked, and who stood there with her eyes closed, said something. She said: "Bühhübel." The Bühhübel was a hidden ledge on one of the slopes of the Hochficht. It was at least an hour's walk to get there.

It was strange how we all headed to the Bühhübel without any further debate. Otti led the way. A bright-red dawn was breaking by the time we arrived. The boy, Ludwig, was lying there unconscious and inert, one foot jammed between a rock and a tree trunk, which must have fallen while he was playing there. The foot was probably badly injured. The tree trunk could barely be lifted, and no one dared to roll it over. Otti took one look and said, "Dig!" Someone had a shovel. Otti pointed to a certain spot under the rock and said, "There!" Just a few stabs with the shovel and the stone was loosened so well that the child could finally be freed.

"She does have something special, that girl," admitted Hochholdinger.

"Magnetic, that's what she is," explained the American Feiferling.

The summer gradually began its retreat from the forest, and September and October were already on my mind. Early autumn was beautiful in this area, the beeches were ablaze in the pine groves, rowan berry clusters reddened, and late flowers were advancing; the air was silent once the morning fog had dispersed in crystalline purity above the varied formations of nature, and the mountain water in the stone trough outside the house had become so cold that you had to set down your cup once or twice while drinking.

"What you writing?" Otti asked me once when I was sitting at the table under the spruces. She'd hardly ever asked any questions before, and her speech had always been terse, except when she was singing one of her quirky songs.

"I'm making something up," I said.

"Like trees do?"

"Like dreams."

"What are dreams?"

"Don't you ever dream?"

She looked at me, clueless.

"When you sleep and then wake up, don't you ever remember what happened in your sleep?"

"Never," she said. "Do they dream?" she then asked, pointing to the heather.

"Maybe. Nobody knows."

From that point on she asked questions every day, and she always began with some word or other.

"Moon," she said, and seemed proud that she knew the name. It was morning and the moon was still visible, shimmering white above the woods.

"What about the moon?"

"Always different." She said it like a question.

I tried to explain this phenomenon to her. She listened attentively and earnestly, but walked away without a word.

I'd observed that for some time now early in the morning, when her day began, she would stand at the doorpost and, using a piece of charcoal, make a mark above her head. There were already a lot of marks there, one right on top of the other. She combed herself before the windowpane in the kitchen, which is where she slept. She took great pains with her two pigtails, and even wove a piece of green ribbon into them that she'd once found on the ground somewhere.

One of the Sundays was the parish fair. Herr Kari had fixed up the bowling alley. In the tavern garden, the veterans' association had set up a wheel of fortune. There were prizes to be won: a "Sandauer" snuffbox, for instance, or coffee mugs, painted plaster dogs, sweets and things made of gingerbread. Three strikes in a row while bowling could win you a ham in tin foil. There was also a *Watschenmann*, a punching doll made of cast iron with a head that barely moved. When you hit him in the face, a hand on the dial would leap up, indicating your strength. In the morning the deacon of Oberplan had celebrated an outdoor Mass. The veterans' associations from the area had marched in with their flags, from Untermoldau, Neuofen, Salnau, Okfolderhaid, Oberplan and, finally, belatedly, from Kirchschlag. ("Typical Kirchschlag," said Hochholdinger.) They were all decked out for a parade. The cobbler Poferl was wearing his fire brigade commander's uniform. Herr Feiferling had a nondescript, presumably American badge in his buttonhole. "You should see how we Americans do a parade," he said.

"How's that?" asked Poferl.

"The drum majorettes out in front dance in the middle of the street."

"Why didn't you bring us one?"

Many people came from across the border in Austria, too, from Aigen and Ulrichsberg, including a Schrammel quartet, which struck up dance tunes at three in the afternoon. Songs were sung in between, and Hochholdinger put on quite a performance.

> Bismarck and ol' Gorchakov,
> One day they took a walk.
> And Bismarck says to Gorchakov:
> You and me should have a talk . . .

That was an old number, in which the Russian prince Gorchakov didn't fare so well.

"Try your luck, Otti," I said at the wheel of fortune. She didn't seem to understand me entirely, but number twelve won her a gingerbread hussar, which she henceforth carried tucked under her arm.

The Schrammel quartet played waltzes, gallops and polkas, and the couples moved more ceremoniously than gaily, even to the faster rhythms. The dancers held each other tightly, but their faces were almost solemnly grave, the girls' heads gently tilted to one side, their eyes half closed. Their skirts undulated like waves, glistening white and foamy.

Towards evening I accompanied Otti back home. We'd lost her father in all the hullaballoo. Behind the village, in the patch of forest we had to cross, the late sun was still shining. There was a spot where the flume took a slight bend, where a path led up to the slopes of the Hochficht. The child stopped there, and I watched her for a while as she listened intently.

"There," she finally said, and began to climb the path. We walked through trees for a while, then we came to a clearing. It was almost dark. She stopped and pointed to the opposite edge of the meadow.

Two people lay there in each other's arms. It was hard to tell if it was an embrace or maybe a murder. I pulled the child away, back down to the street. It was dark now. I heard her sobbing.

"What's wrong?" I asked. "It was nothing," I added, glossing over it. "They were being good."

But she kept on sobbing. It was the first time I'd heard her crying.

"Did you lose your pumpernickel hussar? I'll buy you another."

Toni got home a little later than we did. The child ladled soup into a bowl. But it fell from her hand and broke into pieces.

Sleep came to me late that night. My thoughts of the child held it back. Like clear granite water bursting forth from its secret source, following the pure laws of gravitational motion and earthly order, running its flawless course to the border where human-conditioned misery intrudes! Her mother had apparently taught her some things after all. But the most important things are taught naturally. Something else had then taken the place of her mother, had taken her to its bosom and offered her deep revelations bestowed on no one else; included her in a community closed to others; brought her into harmony with totality and being, so the flower would bow to her and quartz would shine in her hand. It should have been no problem for her to find gold in these mountains. She disrupted class and the Sunday sermon. They'd tried to teach her what was right and where God dwelled, because they knew precisely where. She didn't know; but she existed. Being refused to exchange itself for knowledge, just as agate isn't prone to leave its druse and reveal its stripes, but is forced to do so through cutting and polishing. The agate probably thinks: I no longer exist. But people say: How beautiful it is now! How anxiously she charts her growth on the doorpost! How utterly alone she is!

I walked through the forest more than ever now. I walked through the high-lying valley over to the woods by the lake, the ones described in stories, and followed the narrow path around the lake, encircled as if by a crown of thorns by tangled rootstocks and fallen tree trunks scoured white.

I climbed up to the obelisk in memory of the man who'd stood there once and heard the heart of the high forest beating, as well as the heart of the world, his own heart and the heart of God. I heard the giant stampers stamping and heard the echo of timber being felled.

Up higher ran the border, along the highest ridge, separating secrets from each other, one breath here, another there, a different way of looking, laughing, crying. You walked passed a stone and things became different; why, no one could explain. Here lay the one world, there the other, the line between them invisible and abrupt, like the way a fraction of a second can suddenly divide and transform. I sometimes met Otti on paths like these. "You here too?" she called and kept walking. She must have had her business in the woods, sometimes near, sometimes far; she walked off the beaten path and knew about trails that no one else did, except perhaps for the deer and foxes.

She'd starting becoming sad, though. You could see it at home, in her movements. She hardly ever sang songs anymore. Sometimes I'd see her around the stream, her open hand in the water. The water was icy now, and I said: "Be careful!" But she didn't look up and seemed not to hear me. I saw her hands imploring the autumnal plants, but the plants wouldn't move. She fulfilled her obligations at home, of course, but her movements no longer had the grace and beauty of being in tune with nature.

One evening she came home late.

"Where've you been so long" asked her father.

"Fisher-woman," she said. "Had a question."

I looked at her and saw that she wasn't a child anymore.

In what way does a person die? When his heart stops beating; that's probably the most familiar way. Or by becoming like everyone else. Many people die like that and no one is aware of it, many times they themselves don't notice, their whole so-called lives long; only very late does it sometimes dawn on them for a split second, but they brush it off like a speck of dust from their clothing. When you have the choice you don't even know it, and by the time you know it you no longer have the choice. This is how it normally works.

Stifter Otti was supposed to enter a convent over in Austria. The priest had to twist her father's arm to convince him that the nuns would take good care of her; that she could still go to school and learn something useful; that she was now grown up and they had to make sure she stayed on the straight and narrow; that he'd managed to get a scholarship for her and would pay the travel expenses himself, after all it wasn't that far; that she should thank God for her good fortune, because with a little help from above she might someday belong to the Holy Orders herself or, if God has other things in mind, might lead a different sort of life, one that will still make her happy and which no one, least of all her father, is entitled to stand in the way of. What could Toni have possibly answered, given these many reasons?

He said, "If that's the way it has to be." But Otti lowered her head and said, "No!"

The fisher-woman came a few days later. She'd been a friend of Otti's mother, even though she hardly entered the house, at least not since I was living there. "Mary 'n' Joseph," she said, "just look at this place," even though it looked like it always did, and to my mind rather passable. "This place needs a hardworking woman," she said, and I saw how Otti closed her eyes. Then the fisher-woman launched into a lengthy speech about how the priest just wants the best; she spoke about sin and ingratitude, and what a capital place St Matilda's convent was, she'd been there on a pilgrimage, twelve girls to a room, no reason to be scared, the girls often have a whale of a time.

Toni said, "I've nothing against it." But Otti said, "No!" Tears welled up in her eyes and she ran from the room.

The teacher Macho came too and tried to reason with her. "Look," he said, "you have to make things a little bit easier on your father. No one's going to bite your head off. Everyone's very friendly at the convent. Morning, noon and evening you'll get your meals, they cook the same for everyone. The nuns are good teachers. You have to learn something, you must realize that. You're a big girl now. You'll soon keep house better than Frau Kari does. And if your mother were still alive, she'd surely be happy for you."

But Otti cried and said, "No, no, no!"

No one came for a week after that. Then one day, Otti came to me. I was sitting in the attic at my desk, writing and occasionally looking through the skylight, between the spruces and into the countryside. She'd probably been standing behind me a while without my even noticing, because you couldn't hear when she entered. But this time she laid her hand on my arm, which she'd never done before, and I looked up.

I waited, not daring to say a word in the presence of this delicate creature. I felt her respond to my silent waiting, and when she was ready she said, very quietly: "Should I?"

She stood there and I marveled how much she'd actually grown. Her gaze hovered moistly past me. She shivered as if there were a draft in the room.

"Should I?"

She stood erect and slightly swaying, like a mullein or an iris.

I said, "Look, that's life. I don't know much about it. But it doesn't always do what we want. I know that much. I think it's worth a try. Fish follow the course of the stream, or they try to swim against the current; but they have to stay within its banks. You know that."

"Never come," she said, sadly.

"Maybe one day they will," I said, but I was just saying. "Maybe different than you think," I added.

"How, different?" she asked.

"You have to see for yourself," I said, "there's no way of telling."

I saw her crying. I saw her head slowly wilt on her chest. She left quietly, the same way she'd come. I heard the door fall shut downstairs and saw her walk through the spruces towards the forest.

She didn't come back that evening. Her father and I ate alone. She didn't come back that night. We set out to search and make some inquiries. We searched and asked for days. Then one day the lake gave an answer, lifting her between pale roots up onto its shore.

WHERE THE VALLEY ENDS

I F YOU WALKED northwest from Plöckenstein Lake, downhill through the high forest, after about three-quarters of
an hour you reached a small woodcutters' settlement, there
where the valley basin ends. The settlement was made up
of barely two dozen houses on both sides of the stream.
The stream, not wider than a stone's throw and not deeper
than a walking stick, formed the dividing line between the
two rows of houses on either bank. At the spot where both
rows ended at the bottom of the valley, a footbridge joined
the two branches of the road that led first from the lake to
the settlement, then from there to the village of Neuofen,
an hour's walk in the opposite direction on the other side
of the stream.

Although you could virtually see and hear everything
that happened on the opposite bank, even understand almost
every word that wasn't whispered; and although you might
think that people who lived in the same acoustic area would
be closely linked by a host of other things as well, still it made
a huge difference which side you lived on—that is to say,
if according to the local terminology you belonged to the

right-bankers or to the left-bankers. The village as a whole was called Hirschwalden.

Certainly atmospheric factors played a role in this profound division. The right-bankers, underneath tall spruce trees at the top of the slope leading up from the lake, were more in the shade and only got some sun in the late afternoon, whereas the left-bankers, even though they lived at the foot of a hill, could count on getting sunlight almost all day long. They also claimed to be the older original inhabitants, and had slightly more fertile soil, though the difference was rather negligible, as both groups were basically poor cottagers and loggers with a few goats and cows and this or that patch of potatoes or oats. The forest was ultimately the real and indispensable means of survival for all of them, though none of it belonged to the left-bankers or to the right-bankers; it all belonged to the princely estate, which had installed a forester and set up a forester's lodge right where the two parts of the settlement converged.

The forester's lodge, in other words, represented the neutral and as it were abstract center of the village, all the more so considering that the forester did not hail from Hirschwalden. Though a German from the Egerland, his name was Jelen, at which point it should be noted that the name is actually Czech and means "deer," or *Hirsch* in German, a name which certainly befitted a forester and was particularly well suited to Hirschwalden. The surnames in bilingual Bohemia were always very mixed. A few minutes' walk from the forester's lodge, that is to say a good distance from Hirschwalden, was a mountain tunnel built more than a hundred years before and which the much older, princely timber float passed through; and not far away, in Jokuswalde, was the Bärnstein, a rocky summit where sometime in the middle of the last century the last bear of the Bohemian Forest was shot. This five-minute-long tunnel and the Bärnstein were well-known sights and landmarks of the area.

Being neighbors—and this is true not only for the residents of Hirschwalden, but for everywhere in the world—can make people helpful, but it can also make them brittle and touchy. The slightest indiscretion or weakness or absent-mindedness can disrupt the balance that life in a neighborly community depends on. It's a permanent risk. Now and then you do each other mutual favors, like lending out a shovel or a bucket. But watch out if someone gives the shovel back with a nick in it or the bucket with a tiny leak, which surely would have happened anyway if their owners had been using them, these objects being long in use. The man who asked to borrow it becomes the target of bitter, even malicious accusations that are not confined to the shovel or the bucket. He is careless, doesn't know how to handle other people's property, thinks he can get away with anything, is exploitative, selfish, greedy, and capable of the most heinous deeds. And the neighbor woman who breaks a borrowed jug, even though the jug had a crack beforehand

and although she even replaced it—good gracious—the names she isn't called! She's disorderly, slovenly, degenerate, and always has been; and the jar was no ordinary jar like all the rest, but an especially precious one inherited from a grandmother or bought at a bargain price at an unforgettable parish fair, and no jug in the universe could compare with it.

Such trifles give rise to much loneliness within a close-knit community. Then there are the families: the hearths of love, but also the germ cells of self-seeking group behavior and mutual acts of presumptuousness. On top of this, everyone whom fate has favored just a little fancies that he's capable of doing and understanding more than the others. That which a stroke of undeserved luck has happened to toss his way he expects the others to acknowledge as something he's earned by dint of his superior skills; his better potatoes are due not so much to the quality of his farmland or the favorable location or simply to God's assistance, but to his incredible talent in tilling and cultivating the soil. Added to this is the need to belittle others in order to feel stronger yourself, to savor the pleasure of negation, or indulge the urge for violence.

Over it all, curiously enough, hovers a superstructure of piety which isn't even feigned. For while it is true that the elements, sickness and death spare no one, the mightiest life force is always rapid forgetfulness, that most assiduous reviver of error and evil.

Although the left-bankers took pride in their better haystacks and this or that slate roof they'd installed in place of the straw or wooden shingles, there had nonetheless been a painful counterforce at work for some time now which seriously damaged their reputation: the village idiot Alois. To make matters worse, he belonged to the most well-to-do family on the left bank, the Bierschimmlers, whose name referred to the fact that apart from being cottagers they also dealt in beer, not a taproom, which didn't exist at all in Hirschwalden, but the retail sale of bottled beer. Needless to say, the right-bankers did not get their beer from Herr Bierschimmler, but one of them, Grünschmied by name, had his own beer-selling business.

Now, Alois was by no means a stupid-looking or repulsive creature, but a young and well-developed lad—as if nature had allowed itself a cautionary refutation of the old Roman saying about a sound mind in a sound body. He had never managed to speak in words, let alone in sentences, but had had two ways of expressing himself ever since he was a child: either shrieking with laughter or whining and crying. But the most absurd thing about it was that these utterances always came when the opposite was expected. He mourned on all occasions that were generally considered happy or pleasant, and shook with laughter when calamity struck, if someone was sick or died. In this case he had to be locked in the barn or somewhere else, but even then his shrill, unbroken laughter could be heard from far away in the valley.

Whenever something sad happened on the left bank, the right bank inevitably found out about it thanks to Alois's unmistakable peals of laughter; and if a child was being christened, he let out a mournful wail. If a sudden thunderstorm broke and rain poured onto the freshly gathered hay, Alois giggled grimly, whereas a well-meaning sun was the cause of bitter moaning. Although he was strong enough to pull out a leiter-wagon stuck in the mud, he was useless for any kind of work, for whenever he laid a hand on something, no matter how good his intentions, the effects were always disastrous. If you let him chop wood, the head of the ax would fly off the handle; if he was supposed to hold the door open, he'd tear it off its hinges; he'd lift a sack of potatoes with one hand as if it were a feather, but would tear it open in the process; and he wouldn't carry a crate of beer, he'd hurl it out of the cellar, breaking half the bottles. In short, wherever he set foot the grass no longer grew. Although he seemed well disposed towards children, he could nonetheless be a danger around them, for he always intervened in their little quarrels, and always took the side of the weak or disadvantaged, thus evincing a certain sense of justice, but he knew no limits in punishing the bad guy and had to be restrained lest he'd beat the malefactor to death if the latter didn't save himself by making a hasty escape.

I learned all of this and, as will soon be seen, other things as well, having occupied a room at forester Jelen's for a while, a room with a view of the entire village, both its left bank and its right. I had known Herr Jelen from my earliest childhood. He had once been the gamekeeper in the village where my father was born, my grandfather, the schoolmaster, had taught him how to read and write, and to me he was an important person, a friend who commanded my respect, back when I was a child and would spend the summer in that forest village together with my father.

I'd arrived in Hirschwalden by foot with a rucksack. Coming from the lake that summery afternoon, I reached the right bank whose houses seemed deserted to me. Blazing silence reigned all around, an almost uncanny stillness. Only at the little bridge beneath the forester's lodge did I see a fellow squatting who brayed with laughter as soon as he saw me. I looked around me in search of a reason for this extraordinary hilarity. "What's so funny?" I asked, slightly offended, but he kept on guffawing and gave no explanation.

Forester Jelen, whom I told about this abstruse laughter while drinking my welcome coffee, merely commented: "Ah, Bierschimmler Alois, he's a fine boy, just one card shy, that's all."

During my visit, the latent antagonism between the left-bankers and the right-bankers would surface unmistakably. It happened like this.

The Bierschimmlers' house was broken into one day while the family was out in the meadow. The losses were not that severe, but a freshly baked cheesecake did go missing; it had been on the table, cooling down, and was intended for the priest in Salnau on his name day. Bierschimmler's wife raised a hue and a cry which, thanks to the laughter of her son Alois, turned into a fit of wild rage, which everyone on the right bank heard. The latter felt a certain satisfaction at the damage done to the Bierschimmler woman. They said the Bierschimmlers had had far too little stolen from them. The left-bankers had every reason to suspect Alois himself of having done it, as his gluttony was renowned. Yet Alois had an alibi, having spent the entire day in the meadows where hay was being cut, not actually working but loafing around where the others could see him. So the culprit must have been someone else.

In the course of the evening, Bierschimmler's wife asked the Grünschmied woman across the stream if she'd maybe seen someone prowling around the house, because, after all, she'd been home all day and didn't have any hay to make. Grünschmied's wife took it amiss and replied that no one, save for the cats, would even touch the Bierschimmler woman's cake.

"What?" screamed the Bierschimmler woman, "My curd cheese was mixed with egg yolks and raisins, and even had grated lemon peel!"

The mention of egg yolks and especially the raisins was bad enough, but the lemon peel was more than Grünschmied's wife could bear and made her absolutely livid. "Lemon peel!" she screamed. "Your idiot son might buy that one."

This was not what you might call tactful, and a torrent of invectives followed on the part of the insulted Bierschimmler woman. It was a lucky thing in this case that the stream flowed between them, else the two women would have attacked each other physically. But as if this shouting match weren't enough, the plaintive howl of Alois added fuel to the fire, whereupon the Grünschmied woman couldn't help but get even meaner, exclaiming: "If you get any more bent out of shape you'll end up dropping dead with a stroke and your boy will be in stitches." This still would have qualified as a catfight. But Grünschmied's wife, as might be expected, claimed that Bierschimmler's wife had accused her and the entire right bank of thievery. In just a matter of days, the assertions and counterassertions had become so entrenched and deep-rooted that the left bank took it for granted that the right-bankers were nothing but a pack of thieves; the latter, for their part, accused the left bank of having started the whole affair in the first place, with unknown but surely very evil intentions, to the detriment of the right bank.

The embittered Bierschimmler, whose wife was constantly badgering him and who considered himself and his family to have been the victims of insult and injury, soon resorted to retaliatory measures. He suddenly demanded from Birkner, a right-banker who had absolutely nothing to do with the conflict, repayment of a two-year-old loan that the man had taken out to purchase a cow and to date only paid off in part. Since Birkner was unable to pay upfront,

Bierschimmler demanded the cow as collateral and, when this was refused, proceeded forthwith, while Birkner was out chopping wood, to have the animal driven to his own pasture, even going so far as to have it milked.

Birkner called this highway robbery, and he probably wasn't entirely wrong, and so a few days later a group of right-bankers appeared on Bierschimmlers' pastureland and drove the cow right back to the opposite bank, to Birkner's pasture.

Far from accepting this state of affairs, Bierschimmler threatened to sue and even took the trouble one Sunday after Mass to visit the lawyer in Salnau and present his case. This cost him a full five crowns, for which sum the relevant laws were explained to him, namely, that, while he undoubtedly had a claim to the remaining amount of one hundred and twenty-seven crowns, he could not as yet assert a right to the cow itself, which could only be seized as collateral once the courts had determined that the amount of the debt could in fact not be recovered.

Birkner agreed to raise the amount requested, but demanded for his part that Bierschimmler reimburse the equivalent value of the fifteen liters of milk he had unlawfully extracted during the wrongful confiscation of said cow. Bierschimmler, however, refused to do so, pointing out that, first of all, he hadn't milked fifteen liters and that, second, the cow had gorged itself on Bierschimmler's rich pastureland during the days in question, which is why the milk produced belonged to him and no one else, an interpretation whose soundness one would justifiably be inclined to doubt.

Then one day the volcano really erupted when Alois was discovered on the grazing patch of Birkner, lying under the cow at issue and feasting himself straight from the udder. Now, no one will deny that milk warm from the cow is tasty if not wholesome, but Birkner's wife, a strapping woman who caught Alois red-handed, grabbed a nearby stick and tried to chase the boy away, who broke out into roaring laughter. In doing so she scared the cow. The animal, out of its wits, ran into a granite block and subsequently broke its leg. The cow thus had to be slaughtered.

At that, Birkner filed suit against Bierschimmler, demanding three hundred crowns in damages for the loss of the cow in addition to compensation for the fifteen liters of unlawfully milked milk, not to mention the milk that Alois had made his own. Bierschimmler objected that it's really no concern of his if the Birkner woman chases her cow into a rock, and that he was not about to forgo collecting the hundred and twenty-seven crowns in debt owed to him. The lawyer in Salnau explained that, while Bierschimmler was indeed responsible for the actions of his mentally incompetent son, that is to say for guzzling warm milk straight from the cow, he was not accountable for the reckless conduct of the Birkner woman and its regrettable consequences.

The Birkner woman, for her part, in an effort to bolster her and her husband's case, took refuge in the allegation that

Alois had acted threateningly towards her, what's more had even acted as if he'd wanted to lay hands on her in a rather unseemly manner. Thereupon the Bierschimmler woman yelled across the stream that the Birkner woman was an old frump and that no one in their right mind would ever think of touching her, probably not even her husband, who's been married to her for twenty years and still has no children. The Birkner woman shrieked back: "Better to have no children than to bring a fool into this world!"—whereupon the Bierschimmler woman began chucking stones across the stream at the Birkner woman, none of which hit their target. The right-bankers, in their fury, declared that no woman or girl on their side of the stream was safe, their lives and honor now being at stake. The very next night, a number of the Bierschimmlers' windows were smashed.

The following Sunday, the Salnau priest gave a sermon on the question, "Are we not all children of God?" But the pastor's exhortations were interpreted in completely different ways on the right and the left bank, respectively. Each side viewed itself as children of God and the opposite side as children of the Devil intent on no less than conquering and subjugating the whole valley, which for them was tantamount to the whole world.

Forester Jelen, who'd kept out of the dispute until then, suggested to Bierschimmler that they go back to the roots of the issue and find out who actually stole the infernal cheesecake. But Bierschimmler and his followers explained that it had long since ceased to be about the blasted cheesecake; it was about more important, fundamental things at this point. That was grist for the right-bankers' mill, who now insisted there had never been a cheesecake in the first place, that it was nothing but an invention of the left-bankers, who, notoriously despotic and malicious, were spoiling for a fight and eager to take it out on the peace-loving right bank. And, anyway, forester Jelen, who wasn't even from these parts, should really mind his own business. These were bold words; but in the final analysis the right and the left bank were agreed on one thing at least. It was a questionable attitude, to be sure, because forester Jelen ultimately assigned the logging jobs so essential to Hirschwalden's livelihood. Nevertheless, this occasion revealed the basic animosity of everyone against the estate owners, whose forest with its deadwood, mushrooms, grass, berries and wildlife everyone exploited in his own way anyhow, viewing these as public property unlawfully withheld from them. Moreover, the villagers were well aware that the forester knew better than to deprive them of their logging work, and in purely technical terms was hardly in a position to do so anyway, being all but completely dependent on them in this remote border region.

The Salnau lawyer proposed a settlement between Bierschimmler and Birkner with regard to the slaughtered cow, which with a little bit of common sense should certainly have been within the realm of possibility, but ended up getting nowhere. Because Bierschimmler's broken windows were now added to the equation. What's more, the womenfolk were unable to forget the chain of insult and injury inflicted on each other, and kept on hounding each other however they could. Besides, the controversy that had been unleashed satisfied a deep emotional need on the part of everyone involved.

The latter now included not only the adults, but the children as well. They heckled and jeered each other in every imaginable way, often ending in an exchange of blows, the girls no less pugnacious than the boys. That precious gift of nature—children playing together wholly apart from the world of adults—was poisoned, because even within these rival camps they were no longer free and uninhibited. Some were suspected of defecting, others turned into boasters and braggarts. The loud and ill-natured began to call the shots; the meek and better-natured had to cower and hide. Only the harebrained Alois could break up the occasional fight and calm down flaring tempers; all he had to do was approach them and the presence of this strong, unpredictable boy was enough to disperse the combatants and at least postpone their conflict.

That was how things stood while I lay in the sun one afternoon, in the meadow in front of the forester's lodge. It was especially quiet, as always at this time of day. But this quiet now had a disturbing character, because you never knew if the noisy quarreling of women and children would suddenly erupt again. I lay and tried to read; or, rather, I daydreamed in an open book, in Stifter's *My Great-Grandfather's Notebook*, which was set in these parts. "Read the poet in his land," someone had instructed me once, a correct though not always practicable piece of advice, if you don't want to limit yourself to writers from those few countries you happen to have access to in the course of a relatively brief life. All the same it seemed like a special privilege to engage with the poet of the forest in this valley of all places, even though his gentle law no longer held sway at this point in time.

I constantly strayed from the page, as the case of the left bank vs. the right bank preoccupied me incessantly, and I wondered how hard it would be to bring it to any kind of conclusion and make the combatants understand that you can never actually win a war. For nothing makes the just man more sad than complete triumph, since he knows how convoluted justice and injustice are at bottom, and that even the most righteous person only has half a case before God. That's why no war, it seemed to me, had ever really come to an end; at some level it always continued even after it was over. Because a war is quickly divorced from its immediate causes, acquires a life and momentum of its own. It might be possible to refute this philosophically, depending on whether you view peace or war as the primary state; in the history of human activity, peace has always been a desirable aim but, alas, has never played a leading role. At present no one in the valley of Hirschwalden seemed to be in a peaceful mood, except the forester Jelen, myself and presumably the fool Alois.

Each of us lived in our own separate world at the outer edge of the crater, in which black and red flames scuffled and tussled, and in which there seemed to be no love, or at least none that met the eye. Mother Nature, so the poet taught, ennobles human beings. She hints at what is essential, and all of her endeavors aim to eternalize the ephemeral. Her ultimate and hallowed aim always being life itself, so those with experience assured us, Mother Nature always tends to mutual assistance rather than enmity, otherwise she would be extinct. The pious, believing in a divine plan, have reached the same conclusion in their own way.

How, among the people of this Arcadian valley, who lived in, with, and by virtue of nature, could such a total drive to annihilation emerge for such a trivial reason, sparing only the three outsiders? There must have been an error in my calculations. The greats negated the perpetuation of hatred, and from the fiery-molten vapors of the Montagues and Capulets they had the Phoenix soar in infinite love, the glory of purity and the apotheosis of sacrifice. Maybe the proper thing to do would be to look for a couple like Deucalion and Pyrrha, who ultimately threw rocks over their shoulders in order to create new human beings, paving the way for reconciliation. But it wasn't that easy.

The conflict persisted. No woman spread out her laundry behind the house to bleach it in the sun or baked bread in the brick oven behind the barn without shouting something hurtful or accusatory at a neighbor across the stream. It was inexplicable how so much guilt could have come together in such a small place. No cottager or logger ever missed an opportunity to blame the other side for something or other and make their lives difficult in every possible way. A downright creative ingenuity seemed to be at work here.

The forester had to put up with it, indeed he even had to see to it that the left- and right-bankers, who used to work together in the same part of the forest, now be separated and kept as far away from each other as possible. Felling trees is a dangerous business. How easy it would be for an accident to happen, not always or exclusively the fault of chance or fate; and how easy it would be even in the case of an accidental disaster to see evil intentions and foist the blame on a colleague from the other bank whose only witness was God! But it's almost a matter of principle that God's testimony is only valid for the good. The rest get to know it belatedly.

Something happened at the start of autumn that always happens at that time of year: Someone poached a deer. No one knew who it was, but the forester knew that someone in Salnau had eaten roast venison on Sunday. And, anyhow, a forester always knows the time of day. Jelen heightened his vigilance. But he was too experienced not to know that things like this are bound to happen in a forest and, provided it didn't happen again, ultimately would have been inclined to let the matter drop if he hadn't one day found a note under his door with the name of the alleged culprit.

Now he had to investigate the matter.

"I can't allow anyone to accuse me of aiding and abetting a poacher," he said. "I have a responsibility towards the forest owners. And of course I have a responsibility towards the wildlife, which has a right to huntsmanlike conduct."

It was not just a question of property or unlawfulness. The game population was contingent on ancient, established laws. This order allowed a certain number of animals to be claimed each year, no less but also no more. The right of human beings to presume an order of nature at all might have perhaps seemed contestable; but tradition elevates this right to ritual. That's the way it was, after all, with all orders devised by human beings. Not even the forest owner himself would dare to violate these laws regarding the game population, the former, in the eyes of the forester, being nothing but a temporary overlord in a sinecure granted by a higher power to whom he, the forester, was ultimately accountable. This order, to his mind, was modeled after nature itself, or at least corresponded to the intentions of nature, which counterbalanced or contained an overabundance by means of famine or disease. The lessons learned from the days of yore determined the scope and permissible limits of this order. And the dignity of this experience was more sacred than the arbitrariness masquerading as freedom, however much it derived its claim from a certain hardship. What would become of the forest if anyone was allowed to raid and plunder it at will? The estate owners were no exception, and certainly could not have overridden the forester and asserted such rights by dint of ownership.

All the same, it had never happened before in such cases that someone in the valley had denounced someone else. In their infringements against the princely forest they had always been united; no one had betrayed the other. This too was an almost hallowed tradition. The incident only showed the extent to which this solidarity had been undermined. Forester Jelen spoke about the denunciatory note with sadness.

"And how do I know," he said, "if the man who wrote it—and I think I know who wrote it—isn't the actual offender himself?"

He paced the room, distressed.

"If I let it slide, I'll indict myself and expose myself to calumny. And if I approach the man, all hell will break loose."

"I'll come with you," I said.

It was evening. We went to the left bank. The man's name was Schlehdorner. He was certainly poor enough.

"Don't you want to make amends?" asked the forester.

"And what should I make amends for?" asked Schlehdorner. But it was plain from the look in his eyes that the question was hollow, a way to buy time. Anyway, the forester could probably smell if something was amiss in someone's house.

"You can come up with any excuse you like," he answered, and we left. "What was the man supposed to say?" the forester later said. "But maybe I could have helped him out of it somehow."

The village breathed heavily that night. A final autumn storm had broken. Rumbling cannon fire was accompanied by the clatter of distant lightning. The din came from below as well as from above. The storm poured down and reared up towards the heavens all at once.

In the morning a right-banker was found slain at the edge of the forest near his home.

"The note was from him," said the forester.

"First objects, then animals, and now people too," he added. He was a man of many thoughts.

What else could be destroyed?

At some point or another, human beings first entered this valley. First one, then the other. They were there for each other. They took wives and had children. The forest and their work sustained them, sustained their bodies and their souls. When God existed, the forest was His most beautiful and profound wonder. It was said and written that God existed. One felt it too, often enough.

Then one day, the people became divided. Why that was so, no one could say. But from now on the stream could no longer merely flow, glitter over quartz and granite, make leaves and branches grow, babble through the willows and alders. It had to acquire a meaning: here left, there right! The measure of suffering doled out to each by nature was not enough. Sickness, death in childbed were not enough. The tree felled by the logger, the idiotic son whose language was sobbing and laughing was not enough. It was not enough to be tired to the point of collapse just trying to sustain a meager existence. There were joys and pleasures, there were love, trust and support, but they couldn't withstand the allure of "us" and "them."

Now the courts entered the valley, the officials and men in uniform. They questioned, interrogated, put under arrest. People were turned into witnesses. He said or did this, they said or did that. Everyone was innocent and everyone was guilty, depending on how you looked at it. Long-concealed abysses suddenly opened up. It was no longer just about a murder. Women cried alone in their homes; between crying they cocked their ears towards the stream; and if they heard a sound from the other side, they stole to the bank like predators and hurled the projectiles of their fury indiscriminately at another woman, who had probably been crying before as well. Alois's gales of laughter resounded in ghastly staccato in between—or his wailing, like nocturnal cats or the hoot of the eagle owl. The sound of songbirds had long since vanished. "The swallows haven't been here for years," said the forester.

*

I left the valley on an autumn morning. Sun wove its gold in the misty slopes of the left bank. On the right bank the spruces rose up from their earnest shadow valleys. Cool and melodic, the stream escorted me. The forester waved from his door. No one else could be seen. From an elevation I took one last look at the village, which seemed to be dreaming away in the loving embrace of the mountains, in perfect harmony. Then I moved on. I'm still on the move.

Years later I received a letter.

"I'm alone here, as always," wrote the forester. "But I do have some news. The people are obsessed with politics now. It was never like that before. Are you for it or against it? That's all you ever hear now. They're still fighting like they were before, but in a different way now. The only sensible person is Alois. I've grown quite old and am entering retirement, probably soon the everlasting kind."

That was the final letter from Hirschwalden.

The springs, summers, autumns and winters must have come and gone, but were surpassed by more sinister storms and disasters that disregarded the natural seasons, apocalyptic riders and grim reapers of a deeper, more thorough destruction. And after this came a new power from below, that here too uprooted and expelled the ancestral. It paid no heed to either bank. In the end it forced all to shoulder their bundle. And it didn't rest until the last of them had left the valley.

They had no right to decide for themselves, but who even bothered to ask? The people of the valley could fight each other and make life miserable all they wanted. But it was henbane, pasque flower and belladonna from their own gardens. And these poisonous plants might have turned into healing ones in the long run. Who was entitled to judge? It was their own business what people grew in their gardens. No one could presume to know better and play God. Are we not, all of us, His children? And yet that's exactly what happened.

The valley turned into a no man's land. Someone heard from afar how the farmsteads were falling into decay, the shingles and slates were coming loose, the windows and doors breaking from their hinges, how the storm winds battered the abandoned furniture and broken implements. Someone heard that the clearings were gradually being devoured by forest again, that young spruces were growing rampant over both paths along the stream, and that deer roamed freely between the ruins. Someone heard that an arrogated authority had decided to dam up the water in the valleys where no one lived anymore, creating an artificial lake whose floodwaters would inundate everything, roads and trees, houses and gardens, all that had been inflicted and suffered. And I'm among the last who hear from afar the maniacal laughter above this sea of violence and who grasp its cautionary meaning.

PUSHKIN PRESS

Pushkin Press was founded in 1997, and publishes novels, essays, memoirs, children's books—everything from timeless classics to the urgent and contemporary.

This book is part of the Pushkin Collection of paperbacks, designed to be as satisfying as possible to hold and to enjoy. It is typeset in Monotype Baskerville, based on the transitional English serif typeface designed in the mid-eighteenth century by John Baskerville. It was litho-printed on Munken Premium White Paper and notch-bound by the independently owned printer TJ International in Padstow, Cornwall. The cover, with French flaps, was printed on Rives Linear Bright White paper. The paper and cover board are both acid-free and Forest Stewardship Council (FSC) certified.

Pushkin Press publishes the best writing from around the world—great stories, beautifully produced, to be read and read again.

STEFAN ZWEIG · EDGAR ALLAN POE · ISAAC BABEL
TOMÁS GONZÁLEZ · ULRICH PLENZDORF · TEFFI
VELIBOR ČOLIĆ · LOUISE DE VILMORIN · MARCEL AYMÉ
ALEXANDER PUSHKIN · MAXIM BILLER · JULIEN GRACQ
BROTHERS GRIMM · HUGO VON HOFMANNSTHAL
GEORGE SAND · PHILIPPE BEAUSSANT · IVÁN REPILA
E.T.A. HOFFMANN · ALEXANDER LERNET-HOLENIA
YASUSHI INOUE · HENRY JAMES · FRIEDRICH TORBERG
ARTHUR SCHNITZLER · ANTOINE DE SAINT-EXUPÉRY
MACHI TAWARA · GAITO GAZDANOV · HERMANN HESSE
LOUIS COUPERUS · JAN JACOB SLAUERHOFF
PAUL MORAND · MARK TWAIN · PAUL FOURNEL
ANTAL SZERB · JONA OBERSKI · MEDARDO FRAILE
HÉCTOR ABAD · PETER HANDKE · ERNST WEISS
PENELOPE DELTA · RAYMOND RADIGUET · PETR KRÁL
ITALO SVEVO · RÉGIS DEBRAY · BRUNO SCHULZ